IRON WA

Nate roused himsel⬛⬛⬛⬛⬛⬛⬛⬛⬛⬛⬛⬛⬛ted him to his feet, and ⬛⬛⬛⬛⬛⬛⬛

Pierce and a dozen warriors were waiting. "Enjoyed your little rest?" Pierce asked. "I was going to have you run a gauntlet, like I wanted to do with your friends. But then I got to thinking. I can use you to teach the Crows a little lesson."

"Killing me won't teach them anything about you they don't already know," Nate responded. He wasn't about to submit meekly. He dug in his heels and tried to tear free.

More warriors came to the assistance of those holding him. His arms were pulled to full extension and his wrists secured.

"Not so cocky now, are you, King?"

"Go to hell," Nate declared.

"After you, I'm afraid," Pierce said, drawing his butcher knife. The blade gleamed brightly in the sunshine as he sank to one knee. "I'm fixing to make me a new ammo pouch. And you get to supply the hide."

The *Wilderness* series published by *Leisure Books:*

19

WILDERNESS

Iron Warrior
David Thompson

LEISURE BOOKS **NEW YORK CITY**

To Judy, Joshua, and Shane

A LEISURE BOOK®

July 1994

Published by

Dorchester Publishing Co., Inc.
276 Fifth Avenue
New York, NY 10001

Printed in the United States of America.

Author's Note

Transcribing the King journals is a challenge at times. The archaic spellings and grammar are easy enough to change, but his frequent use of Indian terms and names poses a translation problem.

Consulting the tribes in question doesn't always help because King spelled phonetically, and it is sometimes hard to determine exactly how he meant a particular name to be pronounced. Then too, some of the names have to be shortened for convenience's sake. (Examples: Daunts Him by Blows to the Face, or Paints His Ears and Nose Red.)

I mention this because of one of the individuals who plays a prominent part in this excerpt. His Crow name, as recorded by Nate King, translates roughly as He Who Can Not Be Killed in Any Way, which I have taken the liberty of shortening to the Invincible One.

I hope historical purists will forgive me.

Prologue

It was in the autumn of 1836 that Jacob Pierce became invincible.

Pierce had no inkling of the bizarre twist of fate that lay in store for him on that fine fall day. At first light he started a fire so he could partake of his morning coffee, one of the few luxuries he allowed himself. He donned his low-crowned wool hat, wedged a flintlock pistol under his wide leather belt, and strolled to the nearby stream to fill his coffeepot.

Although the sun had yet to blaze the eastern sky with golden glory, the magnificent Rocky Mountains were already astir with a myriad of life. Sparrows, jays, and ravens warbled and cawed in raucous chorus. Chipmunks were out, scampering madly abroad with their tails twitching. In a clearing by the stream grazed several elk that looked up as Pierce approached, then promptly melted into the dense underbrush.

Jacob Pierce was in high spirits, as well he should be considering he had caught many more beaver than he had at the same time the year before. If they continued to be so plentiful until winter made trapping impossible, he stood to earn upwards of two thousand dollars at the next Rendezvous, more than he had ever earned at one time before. After he outfitted himself with provisions, he'd have about fifteen hundred dollars left. A very tidy sum indeed to add to his already large poke.

Unknown to anyone except Pierce, he had already saved close to three thousand dollars. It was his personal hoard, his treasure, as it were, which he valued more highly than life itself. It was his means of overcoming the poverty that had molded his youth back in New York, his way of escaping the humdrum existence his adult life had become before he left civilization for the frontier.

Another few years and Pierce would have enough to go back to the States and live in grand style. A fifty-acre estate, a fancy carriage, a beautiful, elegant woman—they would all be his. Of such lofty designs had his dreams been composed for the better part of four years, and often at night he would toss and turn in restless anticipation of the good life awaiting him once he traded in his buckskins for city clothes.

At least once a day Pierce took his poke from its hiding place, poured the money into his lap, and counted it, fondling it as he might a lover. The money was all that mattered to him. It was the sole reason he'd ventured into the Rockies, the sole reason he tolerated the dangers and hardships. Few other jobs in that day and age paid as well. Common laborers earned less than a dollar a day. Masons, carpenters, and the like only earned a dollar and a half daily. A trapper, though, earned three to four times as much. Lucky trappers even more. And so far he had been one of the luckiest.

Little did Jacob Pierce realize that his luck was about to change drastically. He sank to one knee on the bank of the stream and lowered his coffee-pot into the icy water. There was rustling in the brush on the other side. Pierce figured the elk were to blame, and paid little attention until he heard a low cough.

Stiffening, Pierce glanced up. Deep in the trees, figures moved. He counted two, possibly three Indians, and dropped flat on his stomach. Rather than lift the coffeepot and have the splash inside be heard, he let go and scooted backwards until he was well hidden. Parting thin branches, he saw five warriors strung out in single file, moving parallel to the waterway. As yet there wasn't enough light in the forest to distinguish details, so he had no idea whether they were hostiles or not.

Pierce flattered himself that he knew all there was to know about heathen redskins. In his opinion they were all just so much worthless trash, to be disposed of or avoided as the occasion demanded. He looked down his nose on the whole lot of them. Unlike many of his fellow trappers, he shunned even the friendly tribes and had never taken an Indian woman for a wife. Some trappers thought he was peculiar in that regard. They simply didn't understand that the only love in his life always had been and always would be money.

The warriors continued on to the southeast. Pierce stayed where he was until they were long gone, then he hurriedly crept to his lean-to and began gathering his belongings. Where there were five Indians, there were often 20 more, and he had no inclination to stay around and risk facing a large war party.

The possibles bag went over Pierce's arm and across his chest, as did his powder horn and ammo pouch. He squatted and pulled the unlit ends of burning brands from the fire, then poked the burning ends on the ground until the flames went out. Thin tendrils of smoke wafted sluggishly skyward, dispersing before they rose higher than the tree under which he had wisely situated his camp.

As a matter of course, Pierce always kept his bundled plews near his pack animals. He loaded them swiftly, saddled his mount, and claimed his poke. His blankets rolled up easily and were tied on behind his saddle. Ever watchful, he gathered the rest of his things, making as little noise as he could.

Pierce was all set to climb on when he remembered to take his special precaution. His first winter in the high country, an old-timer, who had spent more years in the mountains than most, had given him advice on how to live to the same ripe old age. At the time Pierce had thought the suggestion ridiculous, but later, after a skirmish with the Bloods in which his trapping partner at the time had been shot in the gut and died a horrible, lingering death, Pierce had decided to heed the old man's words and do what was necessary to render himself "damned near invincible," as the mountain man had put it.

As yet, Pierce had not had to test his "precaution," nor, if the truth be told, did he want to. He was a trapper, not a fighter, a man devoted to wealth, not to warfare. He would rather avoid war parties than clash with them. And so far he had been remarkably successful in doing just that. Until today.

Pierce took the lead rope to his pack animals in hand and slowly headed northward. He stayed away from open spaces and stopped frequently to listen, troubled by the fact the birds and animals had fallen silent.

From the small valley where he had camped, Pierce made his way steadily higher until he came to the crest of a ridge. From here he enjoyed a bird's-eye view of the surrounding countryside. The sun had risen, bathing the stark peaks and pine forests in brilliant sunshine. He could see black-tailed deer on a mountain slope across the way. He saw a lone bald eagle soaring on outstretched wings. And he spotted the five warriors far down the stream.

Pierce relaxed a little. The Indians clearly had no notion he was anywhere in the vicinity. He decided to wait until they were out of sight, then return and retrieve his traps. The stream was about played out anyway, he reflected, so he might as well go on into the next valley and begin anew. Another valley, another 50 plews. That was how Pierce viewed it. A typical valley yielded that many, only a half dozen of which were kittens.

Opening his tobacco pouch, Pierce filled the bowl of his pipe. Presently he was puffing contentedly, his left leg curled on top of his saddle, his rifle across his thighs. He congratulated himself on outwitting the heathens, and grinned at the thought of the story he would tell at the Rendezvous. With proper embellishment, he could turn the incident into a hair-raising tale that would tingle the hackles of every greenhorn in attendance.

Pierce chuckled at the idea, but the chuckle died in his throat when he happened to glance to his left and set eyes on a large party of warriors on the next ridge over. There had to be 20 or more, and every last one of them was staring straight at him.

Unbridled fear rippled down Pierce's spine. He was petrified, certain the time had come for him to meet his Maker. He noted five riderless horses with the band, and guessed that the five warriors he'd seen earlier were scouts sent ahead to search for enemy villages.

As yet the Indians hadn't moved. Pierce casually upended his pipe and stuck it, still hot, in a pocket. He lowered his leg, gripped the reins, and turned his bay to go down the opposite slope. No sooner did he do so than unholy howls erupted from the throats of the savages and most applied their quirts to their mounts.

"Oh, God!" Pierce cried, jabbing his heels into the bay. The dependable animal sensed the extremity of the moment and broke into a trot. To his mind, unbidden, came all the stories he had ever heard about the many and varied atrocities committed by the Blackfeet and other tribes. He imagined himself being skinned alive, or having his eyes gouged out, or being shot so full of arrows he'd resemble a porcupine, and he wished he had wings, like that eagle, so he could fly to safety.

At the bottom Pierce turned to the left, sticking to open country now to make better time. He glanced back repeatedly, hoping against hope the Indians would let him escape. When the fleetest appeared on the ridge he had just vacated, he uttered an inarticulate cry and goaded the bay to go faster.

The Indians rapidly gained. Pierce was being held back by the pack animals. Burdened as they were, they couldn't run fast for any length of time. Either he stubbornly tried to keep possession of his furs, and lost his life, or he released the lead rope and lived to trap another day.

The first pack animal slowed the instant Pierce's fingers slipped off the rope. He bent low, prodding the bay with his rifle. The Indians whooped with bloodthirsty glee, some veering to claim the packhorses while others, those more interested in counting coup, veered toward him.

Pierce gulped and rode for his life. He had great confidence in the bay. It was a good-gaited horse with more stamina than most. Barring a mishap, he just might make it.

The land became rockier, more open. Pierce saw a canyon ahead and debated whether to swing around or go on through. Since doing the former would allow the foremost warriors to cut the gap even more, he clattered into the canyon, dirt and stones flying from under the bay's hooves.

Jacob Pierce anxiously scanned the high walls for a trail to the top. By getting above the Indians, he reasoned he might be able to hold them at bay by rolling boulders down on their heads. But the walls were too sheer. He went over a quarter of a mile and swept around a bend.

A solid rock wall reared before him. It was 60 feet high if it was an inch, and no man living could scale it, let alone a horse. Pierce reined up and looked around in frantic desperation. He was trapped! His stomach knotted and he felt lightheaded.

The war whoops of the onrushing warriors echoed loudly. Pierce wheeled the bay and raced to the bend, then drew rein sharply again. The wily savages had fanned out across the canyon floor and were closing in on him in a ragged line. They stopped when he appeared, and one said something that made the others smile and laugh.

Pierce was certain he would die. He faced the reality all must eventually face, and inwardly he struggled with himself to decide the disposition of his soul. Would he die a craven coward, cringing from their onslaught? Or would he fight to the last, knowing no one would ever know how bravely he met his end, knowing there was no one in the

States to mourn his passing? He glanced at a parfleche hanging from his saddle, the parfleche con-
taining his prized wealth, and he made his decision. "I'll be damned if the bastards will take my
money without a fight!" he declared aloud.

One of the warriors suddenly yipped and charged,
notching a shaft to a sinew bowstring.

Pierce raised his rifle. He'd expected them to
swarm over him, not to challenge him one by one.
Taking a careful bead, he waited until the warrior was well within range and fired. At the same
time, the warrior loosed his shaft. Pierce was only
able to glimpse the Indian catapulting backward
because he was struck a jarring blow squarely in
the center of the chest and catapulted rearward
himself.

He hit the ground brutally hard. Jarred to his
core, dazed, Pierce blinked and sucked in air. So
that was it, he mused. One measly shot was all he
got off! He looked down at himself, dreading the
sight of the arrow jutting from his body. Only it
wasn't there. He blinked, then spotted the shattered shaft near the bay.

Shaking his head in disbelief, Pierce shoved
unsteadily to his feet. The old mountain man's
idea had worked better than he'd dared hoped it
would. He looked at the warriors, whose amazement matched his own, then at the brave he had
shot, lying dead in a spreading pool of blood.

Pierce saw his rifle and went to pick it up. He
was denied the chance, as two warriors abruptly
roared in rage and sped forward to avenge their
companion. Straightening, Pierce jerked out the
two flintlocks at his waist. He never had been
much of a pistol shot, so he was forced to permit
the Indians to draw much closer than he liked in
order to be sure of dropping them.

The one in the lead held a lance, the second a fusee. Pierce put a ball through the forehead of the first man and shifted to shoot the other one. He was a hair too slow. The fusee blasted, spewing smoke and lead, and Pierce was hit full in the sternum. The impact bowled him over, and he lay in the dirt, stunned. He heard the drum of hooves, heard the war horse stop and footsteps approach. His senses sharpened as his hair was gripped by iron fingers and his head was yanked upward. Above him gleamed a scalping knife.

With a quick twist, Pierce thrust his pistol into the warrior's ribs and squeezed the trigger. The man staggered, clutched himself, gaped in astonishment at Pierce, and died on his feet.

Gritting his teeth against the pain, Pierce stood. He touched his chest, thinking his fingers would be coated with blood, but there was none. His special charm had worked again. He was bruised but not mortally stricken. Yet.

Venting strident yells, the war party swooped toward him in a body.

Jacob Pierce calmly drew his Green River knife and prepared to make them pay dearly for the right to claim his hoard.

Chapter One

Several years passed. The beaver population in the valley multiplied until there were nearly as many as there had been before the coming of the white man. The other wildlife likewise thrived. To an outsider, the valley appeared serene, inviting, yet another pocket paradise in the vase expanse of the rugged Rockies.

Into this paradise rode three new trappers. Like Jacob Pierce, they were attired in buckskins. Each wore a possibles bag, powder horn, and ammo pouch slung across his chest. Each wore knee-high moccasins. Two of them wore hats made from beaver fur, the third a blue wool cap.

In the lead rode the oldest, a white-haired veteran of decades in the mountains, his flowing beard lashed by the strong gusts of wind blowing from the northwest. His eyes were sea-blue, his skin as bronzed and weathered as the skin of an Indian.

Next in line came a strapping young mountaineer whose striking green eyes swept the terrain with bold confidence. A pair of matching pistols were tucked under his belt. On his left hip nestled a keen butcher knife, on his right a tomahawk. Tied to the back of his long black hair was a single eagle feather, slanting out from under the bottom of his hat. With his broad shoulders and muscular frame, he was the perfect picture of masculine vitality, as elemental in his own way as a mountain lion or a grizzly bear.

Third in line rode the youngest of all, a man whose beard was more fuzz than hair. He cast nervous glances right and left and started at the loud cries of birds and beasts. Often he licked his lips and looked at his partners as if for reassurance that all was well. His brown hair was the shortest of the three and brushed so that it exposed his ears instead of covering them as was the case with the other two.

The trio descended to the gurgling stream and sat scouring its length in both directions. The black-haired young giant nodded, then remarked to the older man, "I'd say it's worth trapping. How about you, Shakespeare?"

"This coon has to agree, Horatio," Shakespeare McNair said. "See those lodges down yonder? And up there a ways? A few weeks here would prove right profitable."

The third member of their party coughed to clear his throat. "Pardon me for asking, McNair, but why the dickens do you call him Horatio half the time when you know as well as I do that his real name is Nate King?"

"His memory is failing," Nate answered before Shakespeare could reply. "Why, sometimes he looks at his own reflection and doesn't know who in the world it is."

"Ha!" declared McNair, and then quoted from the writings of the English bard whose name he now bore as his own. "Swounds, I should take it! For it cannot be but I am pigeon-livered and lack gall to make oppression bitter, or ere this I should have fatted all the region kites with this slave's offal!"

The youngest trapper looked at Nate King. "What did he just say?"

Nate chuckled. "It was his way of putting me in my place." He saw lingering confusion in the other's eyes, and had to remind himself that Tim Curry was a greenhorn, new to the mountains and new to them. Curry had not yet learned of McNair's passion for William Shakespeare, a passion legendary among the trapping fraternity. "If you're going to stick with us, you'll have to get used to McNair rambling on the way he does. Every chance he gets, he quotes from that big book he lugs all over creation."

"Big book?" Curry repeated.

Shakespeare twisted and gave a parfleche a resounding whack. "The complete works of old William S.," he said. "The best investment I've ever made. If you want, I'll read you one of his plays after supper."

Nate leaned toward Curry. "Try not to encourage the old rascal or you'll never get a moment's peace." He turned his stallion up the stream. "Now let's find a spot to camp for the night."

The sun hung low in the western sky. Already the shadows had lengthened on the valley floor and the temperature had dropped a few degrees. Nate trotted briskly along, eager to rest after a hard day's travel. He glanced back at Curry and hoped they wouldn't regret allowing the newcomer to tag along with them.

Greenhorns were dangerous, not only to themselves but to those they worked with. Their ignorance made them prone to mistakes, and mistakes in the wilderness often proved deadly. A man might make too much noise or build a fire too big and draw a war party down on his head, or he might not pay as much attention as he should and blunder onto a grizzly or a panther. There were a thousand things greenhorns could do wrong, and did, as the bleached bones of far too many testified.

Nate well knew the difficulties greenhorns faced. He'd been one himself once. But thanks to the patient teaching of his mentor, McNair, he had gone on to become one of the most skilled trappers around. Few men caught as many beaver in a single season as he routinely snared. Few men had tangled with as many hostiles and beasts and lived to tell of the clashes.

Nate was one of the best at what he did, and now he had a chance to help someone else as he had once been helped. Which was why he had offered Curry the opportunity to join them when they encountered the younger man several days ago near Clark's Fork of the Yellowstone River. Since then he had learned enough about Curry to know the youth wouldn't last long alone.

Timothy Curry was from Maine, the son of a blacksmith. He had chafed at the idea of following in his father's footsteps, instead craving adventure and excitement. So when he'd read *The Trapper's Guide*, a manual put out by a firm that made traps, he knew he'd found the ideal career for him. The life of a trapper, boasted the manual, was for men "looking out for pleasant work and ways of making money." The manual had gone on to portray the profession in the same glowing terms as it might the life of European royalty, complete with

drawings that were supposed to represent how real
trappers lived, but were more in keeping with a
boar hunt by an English earl.

Young Tim Curry had blithely accepted the dis-
tortions as the real article. Taking all his savings, he
had headed west without delay despite the loving
protests of his parents. In St. Louis he had outfitted himself according to the advice of a trapper
in from the mountains to "guzzle at the trough of
polite society." Then, in keeping with his reckless
audacity, Tim had ventured beyond the mighty
Mississippi into the depths of the unknown.

Miraculously, Tim had crossed the plains without being discovered by the Pawnees, Sioux, or
Cheyenne. His luck had held as he ascended into
the Rockies, pushing high into the remote regions
where beaver were most abundant. And it was
there Nate King and Shakespeare McNair had
found him after spying his oversized campfire
from miles off.

Just thinking about the youth's good fortune was
enough to make Nate shake his head in wonder.
Most men would have perished long since. He'd
once heard a seasoned mountaineer, as the trappers like to call themselves, calculate that well over
a hundred trappers began each new season, and
less than twenty were alive one year later. Death
was a daily prospect for the men who chased beaver, and only the hardiest survived.

The sight of a clearing brought Nate's reverie
to an end. He reined up, and was about to swing
down when he saw a crude lean-to under a lofty
pine on the north side. Firming his grip on his
heavy Hawken, he rode over to investigate.

Right away it became apparent the lean-to was
old. Pine needles and dust coated the back and one
of the supports was cracked almost clean through.

Nate dismounted and checked for tracks, but time and the elements had long since erased any. He turned as the others climbed down. "Looks like someone else passed this way a few years ago."

Tim Curry walked over. "Injuns, you figure?" he asked.

"No, white men. Or more likely just one."

"How can you tell?"

"Indians prefer conical forts," Nate explained, "the same shape as their lodges."

"Oh. I didn't know. I've never seen a lodge."

Shakespeare was beginning to strip off his saddle. "You will, son. Once the cold weather sets in, we'll go visit the Shoshones. After months of sleeping under the stars, you'll swear their lodges are more comfortable than the finest mansions."

"Are they friendly?"

It was Nate who answered. "The friendliest tribe there is. I should know. I'm married to the most beautiful Shoshone of all."

"You took a squaw as your wife?" Tim blurted out in surprise, and barely were the words out of his mouth before Nate towered above him, those green eyes smoldering like molten jewels.

"Since you're new to the mountains, I'll let your remark go. This time. But keep in mind that some of us don't like to have our wives called that. Only those who think of Indian woman as being little better than dogs call them squaws."

"I'm sorry," Tim said sincerely. "I didn't know. Please believe me when I say I didn't mean any insult." To hide his embarrassment, he turned away and worked at removing his saddle and unloading his supplies from his packhorses.

Tim was more upset than he let on, and not just because of his blunder. It was becoming more and more apparent as time went on that he had a lot more to learn about life in the mountains than he had gleaned from the manual. A trapper's life wasn't the life of ease he had envisioned. Several times during his arduous trek across the prairie he had nearly perished from lack of water and food. The sun had burned him brown. The wind had chafed his skin. Frequently the packhorses gave him trouble. It had been a constant struggle to keep things on an even keel ever since leaving St. Louis, and from what he had learned from his new friends, the worst was yet to come.

Many times Tim had doubted the wisdom of continuing on, yet always he had, goaded more by pride than determination. He had boasted to his family and friends that he would return to Maine a well-to-do man, and he'd be damned if was going to crawl on back in defeat, penniless. His father would shake his head in that way fathers had, and his friends would mock his foolhardy scheme.

Tim hadn't said anything to King or McNair, but he'd tried laying out traps several times before meeting them, without success. On finding streams rife with beaver, he'd lowered his steel Newhouses into the water with every hope of coming back the next morning to find each contained a dead animal, only to haul them in empty. It was as if the beaver knew the traps were dangerous and avoided them like the plague. Yet the manual claimed beaver would fall all over themselves in their eagerness to be first to step into the jaws. He'd realized he was doing something wrong but had no idea what.

Just when it seemed certain Tim would have to give up, along had come the two more experienced men. How overjoyed he had been to have other souls to talk to! He'd gratefully jumped at their offer to join them, and so far had found them marvelous company. The old man, McNair, was a bit strange, and at times King could be downright moody, but overall it was better than being alone. The last thing he wanted to do was offend them and have them tell him to go his own way.

Tim glanced at Shakespeare and was given a reassuring smile. Nate King was leading his horses toward the stream, so Tim said quietly, "I really didn't want to upset him. Will he hold it against me?"

"Horatio isn't the kind to hold a grudge for more than a month or two. Don't fret yourself."

"A month!" Tim declared.

"I was only joshing you, son," Shakespeare said, holding in an urge to laugh. "It helps to make the time go faster if a man has a sense of humor." He toted his saddle under the pine tree and set it down next to the lean-to.

"Easy for you to say," Tim responded. "You've grown accustomed to this sort of life. You must know all there is to know about trapping and Injuns and such."

"I wish I did." Shakespeare sighed, then gazed wistfully skyward. "There are more things in heaven and earth than are dreamt of in our philosophy."

"More William S., as you call him?"

"Sort of." Shakespeare walked to his horses to gather up the reins and the lead rope. "There isn't a man alive who knows all there is to know about anything. Some like to flatter themselves they do, and they let their heads swell as big as the hind ends of buffaloes. But what comes out of their mouths is the same hot air you hear coming out of buffaloes when they've eaten too much sweet grass."

Curry mustered a smile. "You sure do have a way with words."

"There's more," Shakespeare said. "It seems to me that the surest way for a man to keep from putting his foot in his mouth is to keep his mouth closed except when he has something important to say." He put his hand on Curry's shoulder. "I don't often give advice unless it's asked for, but in your case I'll make an exception. I'll teach you the three words told to me by the old French-Canadian who took me under his wing for a spell when I first came to this neck of the country, words that have served me well ever since and helped me to avoid making more mistakes than I did." He paused for effect. "Look. Listen. Learn."

"That's it?" Tim said, somewhat disappointed the advice hadn't been a trifle more profound.

Shakespeare nodded.

"Why, any child can do as much."

"I beg to differ. Children seldom look before they leap, they talk when they should be listening, and they only want to learn when it suits them. Do better than they would and you'll do better in these mountains." Shakespeare made for the stream, wishing there was more he could say, some magical combination of words that would impart his stockpile of wisdom to the novice. Unfortunately, though, wisdom was a lot like money. It had to be earned, and commonly the only way to earn it was the hard way.

Nate King stood by his horses, scanning the valley while they drank. He heard Shakespeare coming and shifted. "Sorry I got so testy with him. I just hate to have anyone insult Winona."

"There's a lot to be said for a man who will stick up for his wife," Shakespeare commented. "Of course, there's a lot more to be said for a man who knows when she really has been insulted and when she hasn't." He positioned his animals along the bank and sank to one knee to take a sip himself.

"Ever worked this stream before?" Nate inquired, with good reason. McNair was more familiar with the mountains than any man alive, white or red. Sometimes it seemed to Nate as if his mentor knew every square inch of the Rockies from Canada to Mexico. Not even the redoubtable Jim Bridger knew them as well.

"Can't say as I have," Shakespeare said. "Near as I can tell, we're in country no tribe claims as its own. We've got the Utes to the south of us and the Crows to the north, but the only time they go through this area is when they're raiding one another."

"We'll have to keep our eyes peeled," Nate said. "I don't care to meet with either." The Utes were a war-like tribe, nearly as feared as the Blackfeet, who had a long-standing policy of driving all trappers from their domain. The Crows weren't so openly hostile, but they had been known to steal from trapping parties on occasion, and had killed a few whites foolish enough to enter their territory alone.

"It's not us I'm worried about," Shakespeare said, gazing at the greenhorn. "We'll have to keep him on a short tether or he's liable to cost all of us our hair."

"There's an easy solution."

"Impress me."

"One of us must be with him at all times. He can't do much harm if we're always looking over his shoulder."

Shakespeare grinned. "Now why didn't I think of that?" He pointed at the water, at his reflection, and quoted, "A fool, a fool! I met a fool in the forest! A motley fool, a miserable world. As I do live by food, I met a fool." His mouth curved upward. "See, Horatio? You claimed I wouldn't know me when I saw me. But if that's not me, there is some-one walking around who deserves to be."

"Your brain is addled," Nate observed. "One of these days someone is going to hear you babble on so and give you a sound knock on the noggin to set your mind right again."

"Though this be madness, yet is there method in it," Shakespeare countered somberly.

Nate knew better than to joust with words with McNair. He stretched to relieve a kink in his lower back, then suddenly went rigid on seeing movement high on a mountain to the west. He looked closely and saw a huge brown shape plowing through a bramble patch. Thankfully, the monster was going up the slope, not coming down. "Damn," he muttered.

Shakespeare looked, and frowned. "We'll have to keep the horses close at night and never leave them untended during the day. A grizzly that size could kill half the string before we bring it down. They're awful hard to die."

"As I well know," Nate responded. It had been his misfortune to tangle with the fierce brutes on more occasions than he cared to recollect, and each time he'd had a closer shave than the time before. Not for nothing had he been given the name Grizzly Killer by the Cheyennes. If he wasn't almighty careful, sooner or later one of the beasts was going to rip him open from neck to groin. The thought sent a shiver down his spine, as if he had just had a premonition of his final fate.

Timothy Curry picked that moment to join them. "What are you both looking so grim about?" he asked.

"Grizz," Shakespeare said, nodding at the mountain. The gigantic predator had vanished into an aspen grove.

"Grizz?" Tim said, puzzled.

"As in bear," Shakespeare clarified.

"As in the scourge of the mountains," Nate amended. "Next to hostiles, they're the one thing we have to always be on our guard against. If a grizzly attacks you, aim for the eyes and then climb the handiest tree as if you were born a squirrel and not a man."

Tim patted his rifle. "I'm not scared," he blustered. "Believe it or not, gentlemen, I'm a good shot. Let one of those overgrown groundhogs pester me and I'll make worm food of it."

"Have you ever fought one before?" Shakespeare inquired.

"No, but I've hunted black bears back in Maine. Killed one, in fact, with a clean shot to the head."

"A black bear is only half the size of a grizzly," Nate pointed out. "And not a tenth as mean."

"Straight tongue," Shakespeare said.

The young trapper glanced from one to the other, then stepped to the water's edge. He failed to see what all the fuss was about. The clerk who had sold him his rifle had spoken eloquently of the gun's stopping power, saying that it could kill "any animal this side of the veil." Buffalo, panthers, bears, it mattered not. One shot from his flintlock and they were as good as dead.

Shakespeare noticed the look on the greenhorn's face, but said nothing. Cockiness, in his opinion, went hand in hand with youth.

Nate also noticed, and almost took Curry to task for doubting him. He held his tongue, though, since he had already give the youth a hard time once and didn't want to make a habit of it. Removing his beaver hat, he ran a hand through his tousled hair and gave his head a vigorous shake. The wind felt cool on his neck.

"Say," Tim Curry spoke up. "Why do you wear that feather? Is it because of your wife?"

"No." Nate reached behind him and touched the feather. "This was given to me by a Cheyenne warrior named White Eagle as a token of his respect after a fight I had with some Kiowas."

"Cheyennes. Kiowas. Shoshones. How do you keep them all straight?" Tim wondered.

"Irish. Scots. Italians. How do you keep them all straight?" Nate retorted. "All Indians aren't the same. Get that through your head and spare yourself grief later on."

"How so?"

"If you don't learn to tell the Sioux from the Piegans or the Mandans from the Pawnees, your scalp is liable to wind up hanging from a coup stick or a lodge pole." Nate hunkered down, cupped his left hand, and lowered his fingers into the chill water. He was lifting the hand to his lips when he spied a stake beside his left foot, buried so deep only the top showed. He swallowed, then said, "What have we here?"

Tim moved closer for a better look. "I don't see anything," he stated.

"This," Nate said, brushing dirt and grass from around his find. "Strange that a trapper would go off and leave his stakes behind. Good ones can be used again and again."

"Maybe he was in a hurry," Tim suggested.

"Or maybe he was killed," Shakespeare said.

Nate had exposed the uppermost inch. He dug further, trying to find a chain. If the trap was still there, it meant the former owner had met an untimely end. Traps cost 12 to 16 dollars apiece, depending on the kind, making them far too costly to be carelessly left behind. Not to mention that they were essential to a trapper's livelihood. Without them a man couldn't earn a cent.

Tim Curry had stepped to one side and was peering into the water. He abruptly cried out, "Look! I'd swear that's a coffeepot!" And then he stepped into the water.

"No!" Nate and Shakespeare warned simultaneously, but they didn't yell in time. The greenhorn suddenly arched his back and screamed in abject agony. As well he should. In his haste, Tim Curry had stepped on an abandoned trap.

Chapter Two

Nate King reached Curry in two long strides, sending a spray of water in all directions. He reached for the youth, but Curry doubled over and began hopping on one foot while trying to get at the trap clamped on the other. Spurting blood turned the stream a dusky crimson. "Hold still, darn you!" Nate said. "Let us help."

Tim heard the words, but they were eclipsed by the incredible pain shooting up his leg. The pain was all he could think of. It obliterated conscious thought. He wanted to tear the trap off, but couldn't get a grip on the slippery steel. The sight of the blood made him nauseous, but even that could not take his mind off the pain.

Shakespeare had started into the stream, then stopped so as not to get in Nate's way. "Pull him out," he directed, "or he might bleed to death before we can get him stitched up."

Nodding, Nate swooped in close, looped an arm

around the greenhorn's waist, and bodily lifted Curry clear into the air. The young man thrashed and squealed, his fingers slapping ineffectually at the muddy trap. In his anguish he dropped his rifle, which would have sunk to the bottom had Nate not snatched it up.

"Set him here," Shakespeare said, motioning at the bank and stepping backward to get out of the way. He could appreciate the young man's torment, but he was more interested in the trap. All beaver traps were not the same. Some were small, some were quite large. Some were barely strong enough to hold an adult beaver, others strong enough to hold a bear—or a man. Some had razor-sharp teeth, others did not. He was relieved to see that the one fastened to Curry was not the toothed variety. However, it was a big one, five pounds or better, with enough force to crack a leg bone as if the bone was a mere twig.

Nate took a step toward shore and was brought up short by the heavy chain. He glanced down and saw that most of the chain still lay imbedded in the muck at the bottom. "Here," he said to McNair, and tossed his mentor the rifle. Then, seizing hold of the chain, he wrenched to rip it loose, but in doing so he inadvertently caused the trap to bite deeper into Curry's ankle and the greenhorn screamed louder than ever.

Nate was stymied. He didn't dare set the young man down in the waist-deep water, nor could he reach the bank so long as the chain stayed buried. Bending, he gripped the slimy links closer to where they protruded from the mud, bunched his shoulders, and heaved. He could feel the mud loosening its grip, but before he could yank the chain completely loose he had to release his hold to deal with Curry, who was kicking and struggling in a frenzied panic. "Calm down," Nate urged, without effect. He gave Curry a shake to get the greenhorn's attention. Curry only struggled harder. Exasperated, Nate did the only thing he could think of to calm the youth. He slugged Tim Curry on the jaw.

The greenhorn went as limp as a sack of potatoes. Quickly Nate bent to the chain again. He had to gouge mud from several links before his handhold was adequate. Then, muscles rippling, he pulled until his face turned beet red and the veins in his neck bulged. The clinging mud was reluctant to give up its prize, but ever so slowly the chain slid free. Finally he had enough lose links to loop them around his wrist for extra purchase. Within a minute the battle was won, and Nate strode from the water and placed the unconscious youth at McNair's feet. "What do you think?"

Shakespeare knelt to inspect Curry's leg. The knee-high moccasins had been sheared clean through on both sides, as had Curry's socks. The jaws had bitten half an inch into his flesh, but a careful inspection showed that the bone wasn't broken. "He was damned lucky," Shakespeare remarked.

They carried the greenhorn to the clearing and propped him on his saddle. Nate got a fire going while Shakespeare filled a pot with water and cut strips from a blanket to use as bandages.

Curry didn't revive until the fire was blazing. He groaned, then his eyes snapped wide and he sat up with a start. "What happened?" he blurted out, staring at his naked lower leg. "Now I remember!" He look at Nate. "You struck me!"

"It was either that or let you bleed to death."

Tim Curry was about to give King a piece of his mind when a fresh wave of pain washed over him. He cried out and pressed his hands to his leg above the ankle. "Oh, Lord! It hurts!"

Shakespeare checked the pot to see if the water was boiling, then fixed a critical eye on the greenhorn. "If you intend to earn the respect of others out here, you can't go around blubbering like you do."

"You wouldn't be saying that if it had been you the trap caught," Tim responded. "I bet you'd be acting the same as I am."

"In the first place," Shakespeare said, "I know enough not to go traipsing into water near a trap stake. In the second place, I've been hurt far worse than you and as a general rule I didn't blubber. Pain is part and parcel of life. Accept the truth of that and you won't be so bothered by little accidents like this one." He picked up one of the strips and dipped it in the bubbling water, mindful of his fingers.

"Little?" Tim grumbled. "I nearly lost my foot!"

"You didn't even come close," Shakespeare said. "Had it been a bear trap, that would be a whole different story. We'd be cauterizing the stump right about now."

Tim hugged his leg to his chest, appalled by the mental image of his foot being severed. "How was I to know a trap was there? Neither of you told me."

Nate was in the act of changing from his wet leggings to a spare dry pair. He looked up and said, "We tried, but you walked out there too fast. You have to learn to look before you leap in these mountains, or one of these day you'll be sorry."

"Who would have thought stepping into a stream would be so dangerous?" Tim whined.

Shakespeare pulled the soaked strip out. "You just don't get it, do you, young coon? *Everything* you do in the wilderness can be dangerous if you don't pay attention. Something as simple as putting an edge on a knife could cause you to lose a finger if your hand slips. Or you might be loading your rifle and accidentally blow your head off. Or maybe you'll go into the bushes to heed Nature's call and forget to take a gun and a grizzly will spot you and decide you look right tasty."

"Surely you exaggerate," Tim said. "It can't be as bad as all that."

"I don't blow about words when someone's life is at stake," Shakespeare said with rare irritation. "I'm trying to help you, you dunderhead, but your head is thicker than most."

"I'd listen to him, Tim," Nate threw in. "The only reason I'm alive today is because I took his advice to heart." He stood, fully clothed again. "I know it goes against the grain to think you don't know it all, but you don't, hoss."

Tim elected to say nothing. He was mildly upset with himself. He'd tagged along with them to learn, yet here he was giving them such a difficult time. What was the matter with him? Didn't he have the brains God gave a turnip?

Shakespeare moved nearer holding an end of the strip in each hand. "This will smart some," he announced. "You might want to bite down on a stick."

"Do what you must," Tim said, resolved to show them he wasn't the pampered coward they thought he was. "I can handle it." He gritted his teeth and tensed, prepared for the worst. Or so he thought. The scalding-hot material seemed to sear right through his skin and sent bolts of fire boiling up his leg. He involuntarily squawked, then choked it off by biting his lip.

"If you'd used the stick, Troilus," Shakespeare casually remarked as he wound the strip around the gash, "your lip wouldn't be bleeding."

"What did you call me?" Tim grunted through clenched teeth.

"A character from one of old William S.'s plays," Shakespeare said.

"Any reason you picked *him?*" Tim asked in order to take his mind off the discomfort.

"The two of you have a lot in common."

"Such as?"

McNair finished looping the material and dipped a second bandage in the scalding water. "Troilus and you"—he paused to swirl the fabric before quoting—"are weaker than a woman's tear, tamer than sleep, fonder than ignorance, less valiant than the virgin in the night, and skilless as unpracticed infancy."

"That's an insult," Tim huffed.

"It just means you have a lot of growing to do," Shakespeare said, unruffled. "As do we all."

Nate walked off to tether the horses. His mentor's bluntness surprised him. Usually McNair was much more tactful in dealing with those unfortunate enough to be suffering from the lingering effects of civilized society. But he could understand why McNair wasn't mincing words. Young Curry had to learn fast or he wouldn't last out the season.

Every horse had to be tethered for the night. Trappers who failed to tie their animals invariably spent most of the next morning rounding up their stock. It wasn't bad enough that horses strayed off on their own accord. Any loud noises, such as the caterwauling of panthers or the roars of grizzlies, might spook them into terrified flight. And there was always the constant threat of Indians, who accorded high honors to warriors brave enough to steal mounts right out from under the noses of their enemies. As a result of all these factors, the trappers had a popular saying: "It's better to count ribs than tracks." Which simply meant it was better to tie a horse and be able to count his ribs the next day instead of the tracks the animal made as it fled or was led away.

Nate took his time. When done, he strolled to the fire and sat down to enjoy a cup of steaming black coffee. Tim Curry lay on his back, resting, while McNair read from his book of Shakespeare. Overhead, the firmament was liberally sprinkled with sparkling stars. A strong breeze rustled the treetops and fanned the flames. Off in the distance an elk trumpeted. The tranquil setting brought a sigh of contentment to Nate's lips.

"It looks as if Troilus will be laid up for a day or two," Shakespeare announced. "One of us will have to set his traps for him."

"I'll go out first," Nate said, eager to venture abroad after so many days in the saddle.

"I'll let you," Shakespeare said. "It'll give me a chance to catch up on my reading."

"You've already read every play three times over."

"I'm working on the fourth."

Nate settled back, looking forward to a nice, restful night. He should have known better. For from the mountain slope across the stream came a guttural grunt that caused all the horses to prick their ears and some to fidget.

"I was hoping it hadn't seen us," Shakespeare said.

"What?" Tim asked, propping himself on his elbows. He'd heard similar grunts before, but had never been able to learn what made them. Wild pigs, he'd assumed. "What's out there?"

"That grizzly we saw earlier."

Tim sat up and placed a hand on his pistol. "Will it bother us, do you think?"

"There's no predicting how grizzlies will behave," Shakespeare said. "They're some of the most cantankerous, fickle creatures in all of God's creation. No two ever act the same. Some will run if they so much as catch a whiff of man scent. Others will go out of their way to hunt a man down." He tossed a new log on the fire. "All we can do is hope this one has never gotten a taste of human flesh."

"Why's that?"

"Once they do, they can't seem to get enough. Maybe we're tastier than most other creatures. Or maybe we're just easier to kill. Whatever, it's a known fact that once a grizzly has filled its belly with human flesh, it craves more."

Tim Curry suddenly felt more frail and vulnerable than he ever had before. In his condition he wouldn't be able to run very far or very fast and would be easy prey for any predator. He stared at the gloomy wall of darkness ringing them and longed for daylight so nothing could sneak up on them unnoticed.

The grunt was repeated, only much closer. Nate took his Hawken and walked to the edge of the clearing nearest the stream. The brush on the far slope was so thick a man would be hard pressed to move through it without making noise, yet the huge grizzly didn't break so much as a twig.

Nate went all the way to the bank and knelt, cocking the Hawken. Although he waited for ten minutes, the grizzly never gave its location away. He convinced himself the bear had opted to find game elsewhere and rose to return. It was then, in a thicket directly across from where he stood, that a bush shook as if with the ague. He crouched and tucked the stock to his right shoulder.

A vague shape materialized in the night, a massive form that blotted out the bush and the lower third of a sizeable pine tree. Nate wanted to fire, but held off because he couldn't pinpoint the bear's head and anything less than a fatal head shot would bring the monster down on him in a flash. The beast moved a few feet and Nate heard loud sniffing. A second later it turned and lumbered into the vegetation, making an exceptional amount of noise.

Nate followed its progress and determined that the bear was moving northward parallel to the stream. He hoped it would cross, since its silhouette against the lighter backdrop of the water might give him a reasonably clear shot. The grizzly plodded on, though, still creating a racket, almost as if it was deliberately stomping the underbrush for his benefit. Then, of a sudden, the forest fell silent.

Puzzled, Nate shifted position a few feet to the north. He remained motionless for minutes on end, until certain the grizzly had gone elsewhere. Lowering the hammer on the Hawken, he walked toward the fire, vastly relieved. But his relief was premature.

A tremendous splashing broke out in the vicinity of where Nate had last heard the bear. Spinning, he dashed to the stream and beheld an enormous shadow disappearing into the pines on his side of the stream. Instantly, Nate raced for the camp, shouting, "Shakespeare! It's coming! It's coming!"

Nate ran for all he was worth. He saw McNair leap erect, rifle at the ready. Tim Curry lifted a pistol, which was as useless against a grizzly as a slingshot. The horses had caught the bear's strong scent and were rearing and kicking while neighing loud enough to rouse the dead. Nate went past them on the fly and stood by McNair. "See it yet?"

"Not hide nor hair," Shakespeare replied, moving so they were back to back and could cover both sides of the clearing. "But I've heard him once or twice."

A loud snap accented the statement. Nate concentrated on fir trees to the east, and observed several shake even though the wind had temporarily died. Flicking firelight danced on the limbs, lending the woods an ominous aspect. He thought he glimpsed a hairy mass moving slowly southward and deduced the beast was circling them. The fire was keeping the bear at bay for the time being, but might not do so for long.

Tim Curry glanced every which way, his arm shaking a little as he tried to hold the flintlock steady. "Where is the thing?" he whispered.

Nate was too busy trying to spot the bear to bother answering. McNair was equally occupied. The horses were becoming more and more frantic, apparently sensing the grizzly had drawn closer to them. Nate was worried that some might break free, so he took a few paces in their direction, thinking he should attempt to calm them down.

Tim Curry was a nervous wreck. He saw shaggy behemoths in every flickering play of light. The fact that neither of the mountain men had answered him only served to confirm his conviction the situation was desperate. So when another crisp snap shattered the nerve-racking stillness, he spun, thought he saw the bear peering at them from under a pine, and fired.

The shot had unforeseen effects, the most immediate of which was the terror it provoked in the already scared horses. Several became uncontrollable. One broke loose and galloped madly into the forest. Another effect was an abrupt series of snarls to the southwest, followed by the heavy crashing of foliage as the grizzly ran off.

Nate began to run after the fleeing horse, but stopped on realizing the futility of his gesture. He had no hope of catching it, but ran a great risk of stumbling on the bear. Halting close to the trees, he listened to the rapidly dwindling sounds of the pell-mell flight.

Shakespeare hastened to the rest of the horses and went from animal to animal, soothing their frayed nerves by speaking softly and stroking their necks. Nate soon lent a hand, and between the two of them they quieted the entire string. As they went to reclaim their seats, Shakespeare saw the stern look in Nate's eyes and touched Nate's elbow. "Let me handle this," he requested softly.

Tim was trying to reload, but his hands shook so badly he spilled most of the black powder he poured down the muzzle. He glanced up and asked excitedly, "Did I get it?"

"With that?" Nate responded angrily. "Mister, you'd do better throwing marbles. The bear wouldn't get quite so riled."

Rebuffed, Tim lowered his pistol, spilling more powder. "Why are you so upset? I saw the brute, clear as day. What else was I supposed to do?"

Shakespeare sat next to the greenhorn and took the flintlock. "Allow me," he said. As he opened his powder horn, he said, "Remember what I told you about looking, listening, and learning? You should have paid attention to us, and if you had you would have noticed that we were holding our fire until we could see what we were shooting at."

"But I . . ." Tim began, and stopped when the older man held up a hand.

"Let me finish, son," Shakespeare said. He wagged the pistol. "A piece like this is no good against a grizzly. Their skulls are so thick, the balls bounce off. And if you'd wounded that bear, as sure as you're sitting there, it would have charged us." Shakespeare paused. "You ever had a grizzly come at you from out of the dark?"

"No."

"I have, and it's not something I'd rate as one of life's great experiences. In the time it takes you to blink your eye, a grizzly can swat you twenty feet or rip you apart with one swipe. And believe me, that's not a pretty sight."

Tim bowed his head. Now that he had a moment to reflect, he wasn't so certain he'd seen the bear. His imagination might have gotten the better of him. "I made a mess of things again, didn't I?"

"We're still alive, so no real harm was done," Shakespeare said, offering a kindly grin. "The loss of a horse will be bothersome when it's time to pack out our plews, but we can live with it."

"True," Nate chimed in. Curry was so downcast, Nate regretted snapping at him. "And I'm a fine one to be mad. You should have seen some of the dunderhead stunts I pulled when I was green to the Rockies. My being here today is proof that fools and simpletons have their own guardian angels."

Shakespeare clapped the youth on the back. "I'll vouch for that. So cheer up, Troilus. Another day, another lesson learned."

"I'll try," Tim said. But deep down he was worried. For the first time since leaving Maine his mettle had been seriously tested, and his insides had turned to mush. He'd always believed he was as brave as the next man, but now he had his doubts. Would he act the same if hostile Indians showed? Would he be so rattled he couldn't load a gun?

Nate had taken his seat on the other side of the fire. He leaned the Hawken on his saddle, then reached behind him to pull the lower half of the eagle feather into view. "Recollect me telling you about the Cheyenne who gave me this?"

A dull nod was Tim's response.

"I didn't tell you the whole story," Nate said. "The same warrior also saw me tangle with a grizzly. He thought I handled myself well. But I don't mind admitting that I was never more scared in my whole life than when that hairy devil came at me."

"You were?"

Nate nodded. "And that wasn't the last time I've been scared hell and cooked. We all suffer a fright now and again. The trick is to find your grit and bounce back."

The youth settled down on his blankets to ponder. Not in a hundred years would he have suspected King of being afraid of anything, man or beast. And if someone of King's caliber knew fear on occasion, he figured he shouldn't be so hard on himself for the same failing. He had to give himself time to adjust, to find his grit, as King put it. Then he'd show them. He'd show everyone that Timothy Curry was a man to be reckoned with.

Shakespeare pulled out his pipe. He was mightily pleased at how Nate had handled the situation. It justified his trust in Nate's judgment, and his decision years ago to take Nate under his wing and do for Nate as he would have done for the son he'd never had, the son he'd always wanted.

For Nate's part, he laid back discontented. The incident had confirmed that greenhorns were unreliable, and some more unreliable than others. He wanted to help Curry learn the ropes, but not at the expense of his life and McNair's. Something told him that unless he was extremely careful, the youth would bring more hardship down on their heads. And in the raw, savage wilderness, where survival of the fittest was the unwritten law for all, hardship had a nasty habit of leading to the ultimate affliction; death itself.

Chapter Three

Nathaniel King spent the entire next day setting traps by himself. Prior experience had honed his skills to where he was a master at locating ideal places and putting the traps where they would be the most effective.

Trapping was never done in a haphazard fashion. There was a science to the procedure that every mountain man made sure to know intimately since his livelihood depended on his ability.

First off, a trapper had to find a stretch of stream beaver frequented. Their marvelous dams and intricate domed lodges were dead giveaways. Then came the next, critical step.

Not many people back in the States knew much about the habits of beaver. Few knew, for instance, that beaver had a way of marking their territory, much like dogs. In the case of beaver, the marking was done by the animal bringing a small amount of mud up from the bottom, smearing it on the bank, and then dabbing the mud with a sticky yellow substance secreted from its glands. Whenever other beaver caught the scent, they invariably made straight for the spot to dab on their own mud and secrete castoreum.

This was their weakness, the Achilles heel the trappers exploited. For it was by smearing mud and gland extract on the banks of waterways, and submerging traps at points where the beaver would climb out to investigate, that trappers snared their prey.

Nate stored his castoreum in a small wooden box he kept in his possibles bag. On this particular morning he had set five of the six traps he'd toted from camp, and was opening the box to dip the tip of a stick inside for more castoreum when he had the distinct feeling that he was being watched. Seasoned trappers knew the sensation well. A prickling at the nape of the neck combined with a tingling in the mind, an instinctive alarm that something was amiss.

Nate knew better than to leap up and scour the landscape. Whoever, or whatever, was out there would duck down and he'd never spot them. No, he continued to work, applying a small amount of castoreum to a large patch of mud, while at the same time, shifting from side to side, he looked out the corners of his eyes.

Waving grass gave the culprit away. Nate saw it move, 20 feet to his left, but didn't let on. He made a show of closing the castoreum box and replacing it in the possibles bag. He still had to establish whether he was being watched by a human or an animal. Standing, he stepped to the last trap and bent to grip the chain. The grass parted, and he was astounded to see the face of a small Indian boy peeking at him.

Acting as if he hadn't noticed, Nate carried the trap to the end of the bank. On the one hand, he was relieved it was only a child. On the other, the boy's presence meant a village must be nearby, much too close for comfort. Should the boy's people prove to be Utes, he would have to alert McNair and get out of there before they lost their hair. If Crows, the situation was little better since the Crows were notoriously unreliable.

Nate had to talk to the child. In order to trick the boy into thinking he wasn't aware of anyone being nearby, Nate set the trap. He stood with a foot on each spring, bent, and opened the jaws. It was delicate work to adjust the pan so that the dog caught in the notch. Then he carefully lowered the trap to the streambed, stretched the chain to its full length, and firmly drove a stake into the bottom. His stake, like the one left by the mysterious trapper who had abandoned the trap Curry stepped in, had been chopped from hard, dry wood. Using freshly cut wood invited failure since it was a favorite fare of the beaver.

Wading to shore, Nate clambered out and shook his legs. He contrived to move close to the patch of high grass. A hint of buckskin assured him the boy was still there. So whipping around, he dived.

The boy was jackrabbit-quick. He came up off the ground in a rush and turned to flee. Nate barely caught hold of an ankle, and held fast. The boy shrieked and tugged on his leg, but he was no match for Nate's vast strength. Holding on, Nate lunged and grabbed the boy around the waist. He almost missed seeing the knife that arced at his chest, and caught the boy's wrist at the last second. The wildcat kicked and clawed, trying to gouge Nate's eyes out. Nate merely swiveled, swinging the boy over his hip, and tossed the spunky youngster to the earth. The boy, groggy, tried to stand, so Nate pinned him with one knee, then wrested the butcher knife loose.

Clarity returned to the boy's dark eyes. He vainly tried to move the big knee astride him, then gave up and glowered, his expression saying more eloquently than words that he expected to die but would die as a true warrior should.

Nate tested the blade on his thumb and found it razor sharp. Tossing the knife aside, he addressed his captive in the universal Indian tongue, sign language. "Question. How are you called?"

The boy seemed surprised that Nate could communicate. He twisted, slapped at Nate's knee, and finally subsided, signing, "My name is known far and wide as the name of a fierce fighter, white dog! Kill me if you will, but know that Gray Badger, the son of Two Humps, does not fear you."

"I am known as Grizzly Killer," Nate signed. "I kill grizzlies, not boys too small to climb on horses by themselves."

Gray Badger puffed his cheeks like an enraged chipmunk. "I have seen twelve winters, white man! I can ride better than you."

Nate held back a smile. He knew that Indian boys were plunked on horses at the tender age of four, and by the time they were ten, they were adroit riders. "Perhaps you can," he signed, "but I can run faster than you can. So I can catch you easily if you try to run off." He paused. "Will you give me your word that you will not try to flee if I let you up?"

The boy's brow knit. "I really am not going to die?"

"Not today. Not by my hand." Nate uncoiled. He grasped the youngster's wrist and pulled the boy upright. "Do I have your promise?"

Gray Badger regarded him suspiciously. "Question. Why would you take the word of your enemy?"

"Even enemies can have a sense of honor," Nate responded, trying to identify the boy's tribe from the child's clothes and hair style. Neither revealed much. Gray Badger wore his hair long and loose, not braided in any particular fashion. His buckskin leggings might have been made by a woman belonging to any of a dozen tribes. The boy's moccasins, however, were different from most. "And I have no reason to call a Crow my enemy unless he shows me that he has a bad heart."

"How did you know I am a Crow?"

"No two tribes make moccasins the same," Nate signed. He stared off down the valley, seeking columns of smoke. "How far off is your village?"

"I do not know."

"Are you lost?"

"A Crow does not lose his way in the woods."

"Then how can you not know where your village is?"

"Maybe I do know," Gray Badger allowed. "Maybe I do not trust you enough to tell you where to find my people."

That made sense, but Nate suspected there was more to the boy's reluctance to answer than Gray Badger let on. He wondered if possibly the boy was on a family outing. "Where is your father and mother?"

"Far away from here."

"Then who are you here with?"

"No one."

"Straight tongue?"

"Whites lie, not Crows," Gray Badger signed indignantly.

Nate was unwilling to accept the boy's assertion.

Gray Badger was too young to be permitted to wander any great distance from a village alone. So either the Crow had lied to protect others who were close at hand, or there was much more to this than met the eye. "Where is your horse?"

"I do not have one."

Now Nate was doubly skeptical. The Crow nation had acquired horses shortly after the early Spanish exploration of the Rockies, and had adapted to them as readily as the Sioux and the Cheyennes. Crows never went any great distance unless it was on horseback. And boys were given their first ponies when they were barely old enough to walk. "Your family must be very poor," he signed.

Gray Badger bristled as if insulted. "My father is one of the richest men in our tribe. He has three hundred horses all his own. And that does not count the many horses he has given away to those in need."

"Two Humps is a chief," Nate deduced, basing his judgment on the knowledge that only prominent warriors owned so many animals.

"My father is a man of great importance," Gray Badger boasted. Strangely, his countenance fell, as if the admission saddened him. "He does not let his sons want for anything."

"Except horses."

The boy's temper made him careless. "Had I wanted, I could have taken any animal my father owns. But I needed to leave quietly, on foot."

"You snuck away from your own people?" Nate signed. "Why? Were you in trouble with your parents? Were you being punished and you did not think the punishment fair?"

Gray Badger lifted his hands to reply, hesitated, then dropped them to his sides.

"Very well," Nate signed. "As you have made

clear, your affairs are not my concern. Go in peace. I wish you well." He picked up his trap sack, slung it over his shoulder, and headed northward, hoping he wasn't making a numskull mistake that would cost him dearly. If there was a village near, the boy would take off like a shot. If there wasn't, if he was right about there being more to this than seemed apparent, then the boy might tag along with him, out of curiosity if for no other reason. He refrained from glancing back until he came to the first bend, and he grinned on discovering the Crow youngster a dozen paces behind.

Going on, Nate debated whether to lead the boy all the way to camp or to try to get to the bottom of things beforehand. He hiked a quarter of a mile and stopped beside a log perched on a cutoff. There he sat, pretending to rest.

Gray Badger had halted. He made no attempt to hide or flee, nor did he approach any closer.

Nate opened his possibles bag and took out some venison jerky. He broke off a piece and chewed lustily, smacking his lips as if it was the best meal he'd eaten in ages. The boy licked his lips and fidgeted, taking a step forward, then a step back. "Question. Would you like to eat?" Nate signed.

The young Crow was in the grip of a quandary. His hunger was obvious, yet his pride prevented him from giving in.

Taking another, bigger bite, Nate made as much noise as a hog at the feed trough, thankful his wife wasn't there to hear him or he'd never hear the end of it. He was the one who always insisted their children eat with their mouths closed. New York upbringing did that to people.

Practically watering at the mouth, Gray Badger advanced. "I would be grateful to share your food," he signed with all the dignity of a warrior invited to attend a grand feast. He took a seat at arm's length and accepted a thick piece of jerky. Rather than wolf it, he bit off a small chunk and chewed slowly, savoring the morsel.

Nate was impressed by the boy's self-control. He finished eating in silence, then signed, "I am with two friends. Our camp is not far, and you are welcome to come with me and share the rabbit stew we will have later. There will be more than enough for everyone."

The boy had frozen in the act of taking a nibble. "There are more white men?" he signed, unable to hide his apprehension. "Are they like you or like him?"

"Who?"

Gray Badger suddenly crammed half the piece into his mouth and chomped down. He gazed at the stream, clearly stalling. "How do I know your friends will be as kind as you?"

"You do not," Nate admitted, "but you have my pledge that no harm will come to you while you are under my protection." He didn't press the issue of the other white man the boy alluded to. All in good time, he told himself. To further soothe the young Crow's fears, he added, "I have a son about your age. You remind me of him."

"I do?"

"Both of you are more fond of food than you are anything else," Nate signed, grinning to show he meant it as a joke. The boy smiled for the first time. "Once, my son, Stalking Coyote, ate a whole buffalo at one sitting."

"He did not," Gray Badger signed, laughing.

Nate beckoned and resumed his journey. Now that he had an opportunity to examine the youngster at his leisure, he observed that the boy's leggings and moccasins were grimy with dirt, a con-

dition no mother would abide. The boy's face also
bore more smudges than regular washing would
allow. The only conclusion Nate could reach was
that Gray Badger had indeed been on his own
for quite a while. But why? What had driven the
boy to flee his own tribe? "Question. Was your
village attacked by the Utes or another war party
recently?"

Gray Badger appeared surprised. "No. Why do
you ask me this?"

"Just a thought I had," Nate signed. They had
to go around a sharp curve in the stream, past a
gravel bar bordered by thick mud. Nate was halfway across when he spied several gigantic prints
in the mud that hadn't been there when he went
downstream. Halting, he measured the length and
breadth with his hand, then whistled in amazement. The grizzly's front paws were seven inches
long, the hindpaws 14 inches in length. The claws
were fives inches alone. A truly gargantuan beast
by any standard.

"I am glad I did not meet this bear," Gray Badger
signed. "He would have swallowed me whole."

Nate grinned to be polite. Deep down, though,
he was immensely troubled. Bears were roamers
by nature, foraging far afield to fill their stomachs.
Often when they encountered humans and were
shot at, they went elsewhere until the humans left
the area. This one had stayed, indicating the grizzly regarded the valley as its home. Bears always
had one place they liked to come back to, a special
den where they holed up in cold weather and bore
their young. There must be just such a den somewhere in the valley.

Nate ran a finger along the bottom of one of the
prints, guessing how long it had been there by the
texture and dryness of the mud. Under an hour, he

concluded, and scanned the mountain flanking the gravel strip in case the grizzly was watching them from on high.

Gray Badger was doing the same. "I lost an uncle to a great bear two winters ago. My favorite uncle, and he was slashed in half, his face eaten. My father and others wanted to go after it and kill it, but he would not let us."

"Who would not?" Nate signed absently while scouring the underbrush.

"He who is High Chief of all the Crows."

Had Nate been paying more attention, he might have attached more importance to the comment. But since tribes often had several chiefs, he let the remark go by. Later he would regret not prying to obtain more information. For now, he hurried to camp to let Shakespeare and the greenhorn know about the bear. The stream widened into a wide pool, and out in the middle sat a large beaver lodge. He hardly noticed, but the boy did.

"Question? Will you tell me something, Grizzly Killer?"

"If I can," Nate signed.

"Why are beaver hides so important to you whites? Why do you leave your own country and come to ours to catch them?"

Thinking the questions stemmed from the youth having seen him set traps, Nate answered as simply as he could. "Our women like beaver as much as Crow women like beads and red blankets. Our men use beaver to trade for things they want, much as Crow men do with horses."

"But why beaver, of all the animals?" Gray Badger asked, still perplexed. "Buffalo robes keep us warmer, bear hides are thicker and last longer, deer hides smell better when wet. Beaver hides are not special."

"True," Nate said. He wanted to explain about the white man's sense of fashion, and how beaver fur was all the rage in the States and over in Europe, but the concept was alien to Indian thought. There was no sign language equivalent for the English word "fashion." Indians were primarily interested in functional clothes, which was why the vast majority wore buckskin shirts and leggings and dresses.

"Then why?" Gray Badger persisted, his tone implying it was of earthshaking importance.

Nate glanced at him. "Some things are hard to explain. The best I can do is tell you that whites value beaver as highly as Crows value buffalo."

Through the trees the clearing appeared. The boy missed a stride, recovered, and moved a little closer to Nate. "Are you sure your friends will welcome me in peace?"

"No one will harm you."

McNair was rummaging in a parfleche. Tim Curry was honing his knife on a whetstone. Both looked up on hearing footsteps and both did a double take.

"We have company," Nate announced.

"So I see," Shakespeare said, smiling at the Crow. "Where the dickens did you find the whippersnapper?"

"He found me."

Tim sat straighter, studying the boy with ill-concealed mistrust. "What's he doing here? Are we close to a village and don't even know it?"

"I haven't been able to get a whole lot out of him," Nate admitted. "But I think we have a runaway on our hands."

"Do tell," Shakespeare said, pulling pemmican from the parfleche. "Maybe I'll have better luck. I speak Crow fairly well."

"You never have told me about the time you spent among them," Nate mentioned. The last he'd counted, McNair was conversant with five Indian tongues and knew another three or four well enough to get by in a pinch.

"My abject apology," Shakespeare said with mock gravity. "Had I known you were supposed to know every little thing about me, I would have sat down long ago and made you a list of all I've done and learned over the years." Twisting, he saw the boy hungrily eyeing his pemmican. "Care for some?" he asked in the Crow tongue.

Gray Badger took a step backward and put a hand over his mouth, expressing astonishment.

"Yes, I know your language," Shakespeare went on amiably. "It is one of the easiest tongues for white men to learn. We can use it without twisting our tongues into knots." He took a bite of the pemmican, a popular Indian food made by pounding dry meat to a fine consistency and mixing it with melted animal fat.

Nate guessed what McNair was up to and commented, "I've already fed him jerky."

"Oh?" Shakespeare held out the pemmican and the boy snatched it. "I haven't met a coon his age yet who doesn't have a bottomless pit for a stomach."

Tim Curry was troubled and voiced his feelings. "Should we be doing this? What if he was sent by a war party to spy on us? For all we know there are hordes of braves lurking in the woods right this instant, waiting for this boy's signal before they pounce."

"You missed your calling, Troilus," Shakespeare responded. "With the imagination you have, you should be a fiction writer like James Fenimore Cooper instead of a trapper."

"I'm serious. I've heard tell Indians try tricks like this."

Shakespeare slowly stood. "Your life will be a whole lot happier, son, if you believe only half of what you see and a third of what you hear."

Annoyed at being taken so lightly, Tim turned away and folded his arms across his chest. "Fine," he said. "Treat me like an idiot. But don't say I didn't warn you when we're set upon and wind up being burned at the stake."

Neither Nate nor McNair felt compelled to inform the greenhorn that they had never heard of a single instance in which a white man had met his end in that particular manner. Nate poured himself a cup of coffee while Shakespeare watched the famished boy eat.

"What are we going to do?" Nate inquired. "We can't just keep him around. Sooner or later a search party is bound to show up." He took a sip. "If only we knew what brought him to the valley."

"Let's find out," Shakespeare said, and switched to the Crow language. "We are very curious, my young friend. We would like to know what you are doing here. And where we can find your village."

The boy had been chewing heartily. He stopped, suddenly downcast, and fixed his gaze on the ground. "If I tell you, you will make me go back. He will be mad and punish me. I will be beaten."

"Who will? Your father?" Shakespeare asked, convinced the boy was lying. Many years ago he'd spent two winters living with Crows and learned that it was against tribal custom for parents to use corporal punishment on their children.

"No. Invincible One will order it done."

"Is that the name of your chief?"

"It is the name . . ." Gray Badger began, lifting his head, and abruptly stopped, fear lining his smooth features as he looked over McNair's right shoulder.

Shakespeare spun, dreading the grizzly had returned. Instead, he found the clearing partially ringed by a score of somber Crow warriors.

Chapter Four

Nate King was in the act of removing six traps from a pack so he could set them later in the day when he heard the boy's sharp intake of breath. He glanced up, then swiftly rose, his Hawken in hand. As yet none of the Crows had brought a weapon to bear, but their expressions did not bode well. Sidling closer to the sulking greenhorn, he nudged Curry with a toe.

"What do you want?" Tim asked brusquely while staring off in space.

"We have more visitors."

Tim shifted, cursed, and went for one of his pistols. His hand was closing on the butt when Nate's hand clamped on his shoulder.

"Don't be a fool. There are too many. They'd fill us full of arrows before you got off a shot."

"What do we do, then?" Tim whispered.

"We let them make the first move," Nate said, "and pray to high heaven they're friendly."

"Maybe we should make a run for it," Tim proposed. "If we can get to the horses before they do, they'll never catch us. They're all on foot."

"You're not up to running with your ankle in the shape it is," Nate reminded him. "And for all we know, their mounts are back in the trees."

"We can't just do nothing!"

"That's exactly what we will do," Nate said. "We don't want to provoke them if we can avoid it. We have too much to lose."

"Don't worry on my account."

"I was thinking of the horses and all our gear." Nate took a step to the left so he would have a clear shot as the Crows warily advanced. He pegged a stocky man with an arrogant strut as the leader of the band, and he didn't care for the way the man openly sneered at them.

Shakespeare's rifle lay propped on his saddle. He edged toward it while proclaiming, "Greetings to our Crow brothers! Come, join us for coffee and pemmican. There is plenty to go around."

On hearing their own tongue, the Crows halted to a man. The stocky brave, who held a fusee, cocked his head and demanded, "Who are you, white man, and how do you know our tongue?"

"My Indian name is Wolverine," Shakespeare disclosed, "and I learned the ways of the Crows when I lived among the people of the great chief Long Hair many winters ago."

"Many is right," the spokesman declared. "Long Hair was killed by Blackfeet when I was half the age I am now." He touched his chest. "I am called Whirlwind Hawk."

"You are welcome at our fire."

Whirlwind Hawk motioned, and all the Crows came several feet nearer. None made any threatening gestures. Neither did they smile or give any other indication of being overly friendly.

Nate grew uneasy. Not only did he have no idea what was being said, he was now hemmed in on three sides and there were too many warriors for him to hold at bay with just three guns. Moving so that his back was to the fire, he tried to keep them all in sight at once.

"You have done us a favor, Wolverine," Whirlwind Hawk told Shakespeare, and pointed at the boy. "We have been searching for Gray Badger for six sleeps. His father will be pleased to have him back."

"Is his father named Invincible One?"

Whirlwind Hawk scowled. "No. Two Humps." He paused. "What did the boy tell you about Invincible One?"

"Only his name. Is he a chief?"

"Invincible One rules our people."

"Interesting," Shakespeare said. "I thought I knew all the high chiefs of the Crow nation by name if not on sight, and yet I have never heard of this man."

"Invincible One is not chief of all the Crows. He is chief of our village alone."

"Your chief has a very unusual name."

"Invincible One is a very unusual man," Whirlwind Hawk said. Again he took a few steps, and at his cue so did the rest. A mere six feet separated the crescent of Crows from the three free trappers.

Nate fingered the hammer of his rifle. "Shakespeare," he interrupted, "I don't like this one bit. What do they want? Are they after the boy?"

McNair turned to answer, and Whirlwind Hawk chose that moment to yip like a coyote. At the signal all the warriors sprang forward. So swift was their attack that they were on the vastly outnumbered trappers before a shot could be fired.

Nate King tried. He brought the Hawken up and was leveling it at one of the braves when he was rammed into by two more, one tackling him low, the other catching him in the chest with a stony shoulder. Nate tumbled backwards, losing his grip on the Hawken. With a start he realized he was falling into the fire, and he threw himself to the right to escape the flames. The Indian holding his legs let out a squawk and let go, allowing Nate to scramble to his knees as more warriors swarmed in.

Nate had a glimpse of Shakespeare fighting madly and Tim Curry being overwhelmed by four adversaries. Then he had to devote all his energy to preserving his own life. A warrior grabbed his left arm and he buried his right fist in the man's stomach. Another Crow pounced on him from behind, looping an arm about his neck. Nate bent, flipping the man clear over him into another onrushing brave.

Momentarily free, Nate rose and tried to unlimber his tomahawk. He was set upon by two assailants who grabbed his shoulders in order to fling him to the ground. Nate planted knuckles on the mouth of one, then kicked the other in the knee. Both crumpled.

Ducking under an awkward punch thrown by a skinny Crow, Nate retaliated with a sweeping right cross that rocked the man on his heels. He landed another blow to the midsection of a warrior, who staggered aside. Skipping to the left, Nate suddenly realized that not one of his attackers had relied on a weapon. There could only be one explanation: The Crows wanted to take them alive! Already Tim Curry was down and being bound at the wrists. Nate couldn't see Shakespeare, but from the commotion McNair was putting up one hell of a fight.

Suddenly Whirlwind Hawk himself appeared. He barked words that Nate didn't understand, then launched himself at Nate with both arms extended. Nate slipped out of the way, seized Whirlwind Hawk's wrist, and swung with all his might, flinging the stocky warrior into two others.

Pivoting, Nate spied his Hawken and started for it. A Crow was faster. Since further resistance would result in certain capture, Nate decided to make a break for it and come back to help his friends later. He sprinted toward the horses, going less than ten feet when he was overhauled by several fleet warriors. Hands gripped his shirt, his arm, his right leg.

The ground leaped up at Nate's face. He managed to twist so that his shoulder bore the brunt of the impact. Then he was on one knee and slugging fiercely, raining punches on Crow after Crow, dropping one after another only to have more take their place. He shoved to his feet, was hit low in the back. Pain lancing his spine, he spun and clipped the man responsible on the chin.

From all directions at once sped more Crows. Six, seven, eight warriors buried Nate under their combined weight. He punched, kicked, pumped his elbows into faces and necks. Crows grunted, cried out, roared in frustration. Iron fingers found his wrists and ankles and held on. Gradually his strength ebbed and his limbs were pinned. He looked up at a circle of bloody, battered faces.

Shakespeare McNair still fought on. Not for nothing had the Flatheads named him Wolverine decades ago when he first came to the vast Rockies. He had been one of the first white men to set foot in the pristine realm the Indians called home, and all the tribes had been impressed by the strange newcomer whose honesty was beyond reproach and whose savagery in battle was memorable.

Few of the current crop of hardy free trappers knew much about Shakespeare's past. The same even applied to Nate, who had been taken into the mountain man's confidence. Most had heard stories circulated by Indians belonging to the four tribes who claimed McNair had lived among them at one time or another. Of his early exploits, the most persistent were about his prowess in battle.

Many of the younger trappers rated the tales as so much nonsense. They would hear of the time Shakespeare supposedly slew eight Bloods in personal combat using nothing but a tomahawk, and they would look at the white-haired legend with his slightly drooped shoulders and seamed features and would shake their heads in wry amusement.

But the stories were true, as the Blackfoot Confederacy, the Comanches, and the Apaches could all attest. McNair was the most peaceable of men most of the time. Until riled. Then he transformed himself into a raging wolverine.

This day the Crows were finding it out the hard way. Strive as they might, they couldn't subdue McNair. Despite his years, he was panther-quick and coiled steel. Hitting and kicking and gouging and biting, he held them off. Slippery as an eel and as sinuous as a snake, he slipped out of their grasp again and again.

Only four Crows had converged on him at the outset of the fight. He was the oldest, Whirlwind Hawk had reasoned when spying on the whites from the brush, so he would be the easiest to capture. But it was the youngest trapper who had succumbed first after hardly offering any resistance. The next oldest had put up a terrific struggle, but now was bound. Leaving only the old man, who put the Crows to shame with his tenacity.

At a command from Whirlwind Hawk, all the warriors except for two formed a circle around Shakespeare. Whirlwind Hawk wiped a trickle of blood from his throbbing bottom lip, then held his hand aloft. "Will you come quietly now, Wolverine? You have my word that you will not be harmed."

Shakespeare McNair was covered with sweat and panting heavily. The exertion had drained him of energy, sapped his vitality. He girded his reservoir of stamina and straightened, adopting a grim front for the benefit of the Crows. "You expect me to trust a man who took advantage of our hospitality and attacked us without reason? You have no honor, and the Blanket Chief will know as much when he finds we have been made prisoners."

"The Blanket Chief is in this area?"

"He is, with sixty others," Shakespeare lied with a straight face. He referred to the one trapper nearly all Indians knew, Jim Bridger, whose firm dealings with them on behalf of the Rocky Mountain Fur Company had earned him a widespread reputation as a man of integrity and courage. Actually, Shakespeare had no idea where Bridger had elected to trap that season. For all he knew, Bridger's brigade was hundreds of miles away. But the Crows would be less likely to do anything to Nate, Curry, and him if they thought a whole company of vengeful trappers would swoop down on their village in retaliation.

"Where is the Blanket Chief's camp?" Whirlwind Hawk wanted to know.

"On the moon."

"We will find out in time. You might as well tell us now."

"And deprive you of all that hard work?" Shakespeare forced a laugh. "I hope you do find him. The Blanket Chief is smarter than I am. He will not fall for the same trick. Your bones will be left for the vultures to pick clean."

"You are a fool, old one."

"And you are a lying pile of buffalo droppings."

Whirlwind Hawk flashed his arm downward. The warriors charged, coming from every direction, too many for any one man to withstand no matter how strong or crafty or slippery he might be. Shakespeare was literally buried under bronzed bodies.

Nate King saw and tried to stand, to go to his mentor's aid. His wrists were tied behind his back, but his legs were free. He was halfway erect when the sharp tip of a lance jabbed into his side. The muscular Crow beside him grunted and gestured for him to sit back down.

Resentment coursing red-hot through his veins, Nate was on the verge of lashing out when he realized he would be endangering himself needlessly. It was too late to help Shakespeare, who was being trussed up. Nate sank to his knees and held his anger in check. He made a mental vow that come what may, he was going to see the Crows pay for their vile deceit.

The band swiftly prepared to depart. Packs and plews were tied on horses. Nate, Shakespeare, and Tim were hoisted on mounts, each with personal guards who led their animals by the reins. All was in readiness when an argument broke out among the Crows.

"What is the racket all about?" Nate asked McNair.

"They're squabbling over which one of them is the biggest jackass," Shakespeare said, and chuckled. "In all the confusion, the boy vamoosed."

Only then did Nate realize Gray Badger was missing. He was glad, for the boy's sake. Gray Badger couldn't have much of a father if Two Humps let others hunt the boy down instead of doing it himself.

There was a delay while the Crows spread into the surrounding forest in search of the runaway. Young Tim Curry watched them go, then slumped in abject misery, certain his end was near. His quest for excitement seemed a deluded craving in light of the harsh reality of wilderness life. He remembered how his family had warned him he would suffer just such a fate if he was foolhardy enough to travel beyond the frontier, remembered laughing at them and assuring them he was capable of dealing with "ignorant heathens and dumb beasts." Little had he known.

Within half an hour the warriors returned empty-handed. Whirlwind Hawk led the party to a meadow a hundred yards away where the Crows had left their war horses. There the warriors huddled and argued in low tones. Presently half the band was trotting to the northeast with the prisoners while the rest stayed to continue to look for the boy.

Nate was pleased. Now there were only ten Crows. He had been secretly working at his bounds, alternately straining against them and letting his wrists go limp, and had loosened the loops a little. Not enough to slip free yet, or to seize the reins and ride off. The thought caused a thrill to shoot through him. He didn't need his hands to ride. A skilled horsemen could control a mount using leg pressure alone. He looked at the warrior leading his horse. The man held the rope lightly, carelessly. It would be child's play.

Nate bided his time for over an hour. They had just started down the slope of a jagged mountain after negotiating a high pass when he put his plan into effect. The warrior in front of him went around a large boulder and for a moment was out of sight. The warrior behind him had lagged a dozen yards. There might never be a better opportunity.

Nate jammed his heels into his horse and the animal took off, racing around the boulder and breaking into a gallop as soon as it was in the clear. He bent low, guiding the sorrel with his knees. He saw the warrior holding the rope twist and try to tighten his grip, but the fleeing horse ripped it loose, tearing off skin in the process.

Strident yells erupted. Nate angled toward thick timber and reached the tree line as an arrow nipped a branch to his left. Eight of the Crows were in pursuit, two with bows raised. Nate plunged into underbrush, cut to the right, covered 50 yards, then cut to the left, down slope. Low limbs tore at his face, his shoulders. One scratched his cheek, drawing blood. He had to clamp his legs hard against the animal's sides to keep from being pitched off.

The Crows were howling like incensed wolves. They had spread out and the fleetest were trying to get ahead of him to cut him off.

Nate desperately tugged at his bounds. He could only go so fast without his hands. In order to escape he must break free. The rope bit into his flesh, slicing the skin. He felt blood, and smiled grimly. Blood would make his wrists slippery, would hasten his release. He redoubled his efforts.

A Crow warrior closed rapidly on the right. The man rode a superb paint that skirted trees and leaped logs at breakneck speed. Grinning in antici- pation, the warrior hefted a war club, anxious to be the one to bring the white man down.

Nate was making painful but steady progress on the ropes. He turned his wrists furiously, the loops chafing deeper and deeper, the blood flowing thickly. Suddenly his left wrist jerked loose and he swung both hands in front of him to seize the sorrel's mane. None too soon.

The warrior with the war club roared in feral delight as he broke from a thicket not ten yards away. Waving the club overhead, he raced alongside the sorrel.

Nate ducked under a vicious swing that would have caved in his skull like an overripe gourd. The Crow raised the club for another swing. Shifting, Nate kicked, driving his foot into the man's chest. The blow sent the warrior flying from the paint; he let out a yip as he collided with a prickly pine.

Inspiration struck Nate even as the Crow fell. For several fleeting seconds the paint brushed against the sorrel, and in that span he tensed all his limbs and pushed off from the sorrel's back. The paint began to pull ahead and for a few anxious moments Nate thought he would tumble earthward. Then he came down astride the Crow's mount, gripped the trailing reins, and applied both heels.

In a burst of speed the paint streaked past the sorrel. Nate veered to the right to avoid a fir tree. A meadow unfolded before him. He was a third of the way across when two Crows appeared behind him, side by side, one with a bow.

Nate reined sharply to the left as a glittering shaft sought his back. The arrow missed by yards. Nate reined in the opposite direction and kept on weaving until he regained cover. The Crows gradually lost ground, their inferior mounts unable to sustain the pace.

Renewed confidence brought a smile to Nate's lips. He would eventually lose his pursuers, then circle around to pick up the war party's trail. From there on, he would stalk them until he could free Shakespeare and Curry.

The timber thinned little by little. More and more boulders dotted the mountainside. Nate wasn't worried because he was well beyond bow range. The Crows didn't have a prayer of catching him. Or so he thought until a cliff reared directly ahead.

Nate slowed, scouring the barrier. It seemed to extend endlessly on either hand. He knew there had to be a break somewhere, so he bore to the left and hugged the base for the next half a mile. Repeatedly he checked his back trail without seeing sign of the Crows. He had about accepted that they had given up when wisps of dust hovering in the afternoon air showed otherwise. They were five or six hundred yards off, and closing.

Below Nate lay a steep, barren slope littered with small boulders and loose gravel. He couldn't go that way. The footing would be too treacherous and there was no cover. No, he had to reach the end of the cliff, and do it quickly. Whipping the paint with the reins and pumping his legs, he galloped along until the barrier was abruptly replaced by the narrow mouth of a canyon.

Nate didn't like the notion of entering, but he had no choice. The Crows were much nearer, the slope below still open. Stones clattering under the paint's hoofs, Nate wound into the depths of the canyon. High walls shaded him from the sun. Occasionally he saw massive boulders perched on the rims, and hoped they wouldn't come crashing down on top of him.

One thing was encouraging. Nate found dozens of animal tracks, proof wildlife passed through on a regular basis. There must be a way out, he figured.

The canyon floor climbed. Nate looked back often but as yet couldn't see the Crows. The dust now hung in the canyon so they had to be close. He wished he had a weapon, any weapon. The warriors had stripped him of everything, including his possibles bag. Making a fire would be no problem since he could do without his flint and steel, but bagging game would be a challenge. To say nothing of defending himself if the Crows caught him.

The walls became shorter the higher Nate ascended. Soon he could hear the echoes of hoofbeats from below. He came to a wide shelf where a waist-high boulder sat near the edge, and drew rein. Swinging off, he ran to the boulder and knelt. It appeared to weigh upwards of two hundred pounds, only a bit more than he did. Bracing himself, Nate pushed and moved it a few inches. It was much heavier than he has estimated, more like three hundred. Digging in his moccasins, he tried again, his muscles quivering as he strained to his utmost. Slowly the boulder slid, inch by laborious inch, to the edge of the shelf.

Suddenly the Crows rode into view, a lanky warrior at the forefront scouring the ground, reading his tracks. Nate braced both feet, wedged his fingers as far under the boulder as they would go, and heaved. With a resounding thud the boulder flipped onto the incline and rolled downward, gaining momentum as it went.

The Crows heard and glanced up. Instantly they wheeled and fled, trying to reach the first bend before the boulder brought one of them low. All but one gained safety. The last man was mere yards from the turn when the heavy projectile rammed into the back of his horse and the animal spilled earthward, dumping the Crow.

Nate didn't wait to see the result. He had bought himself a few minutes, at most, and he meant to take advantage of them. Rising, he whirled, and his heart missed a beat. For the crash of the boulder had sent the paint fleeing on up the canyon. He was afoot, unarmed, and hemmed in by the canyon walls. In short, he was as good as dead!

Chapter Five

Nate King rose and sprinted after the paint. He went 20 yards before it sank in that he'd need the speed of an antelope to catch the fleeing horse. Giving up, he turned and ran to the rim of the shelf. The Crows were gathered around their fallen fellow, tending his broken, bloody body.

Moving back so they wouldn't spot him, Nate cast about for a means out of his predicament. The rock walls were too sheer and smooth to scale. Nor were there any large boulders to hide behind. Once the warriors swept over the rim, he wouldn't last five seconds.

Then Nate's gaze drifted to the bottom of the wall to his right and a spark of hope was kindled in his breast. Carved out of the rock by the wear and tear of erosion over countless years was a niche approximately five feet in length and three feet wide. Nate dashed over and hunkered down for a closer look. There was barely enough room

71

for him if he contorted himself just right.

Harsh yells heralded the oncoming Crows. Nate dropped onto his right side with his back to the opening and scooted into the niche, wriggling to squeeze his wide shoulders under the upper lip. Rough stone scraped his skin, gouging flesh. He put both hands flat and squirmed and shoved until his buttocks touched.

Nate could only hope that none of the Crows looked down as they streaked past or they might catch a glimpse of him. The hammering of hoofs pealed off the walls. He swore the ground under him shook when the leading riders rushed into sight. From where Nate lay, all he could see were the legs of horses, yet he dared not peek out. He'd be wholly at their mercy if they found him.

At a full gallop the war party sped on up the canyon. Only when the last warrior had disappeared did Nate crawl out and stand. Now he had to reach the canyon mouth before the Crows overtook the paint and discovered they had been duped.

Breaking into a run, Nate went down the incline. The warrior thrown by the horse was sprawled in a spreading pool of blood that seeped from a nasty gash in his chest. The cause of death, however, had been a broken neck. The man's head was bent at an unnatural angle, his tongue sticking between his parted teeth.

Nate was more interested in the warrior's weapons. In their haste to overtake him, the rest had ridden off without stripping the dead brave's knife and tomahawk. Both Nate hurriedly appropriated. Then he rose and ran to the bend. He doubted that he'd be able to reach the mouth before the Crows returned, but he wasn't about to give up so long as breath remained in his body.

Nate raced around the bend, and had to leap to

the right to avoid colliding with the dead brave's mount. The horse stood with head low, more shaken than battered by its fall. Bleeding cuts marred its legs and flanks, and its hind end had been bashed badly by the boulder. Otherwise, it appeared fine. There were no broken bones that Nate could find, so, seizing the reins, he vaulted astride the dazed animal and prodded it down the canyon at a canter.

Nate didn't look back until he was almost out. Reining up, he twisted and spied the Crows on a ridge adjacent to the canyon. They had seen him and were waving their lances and bows in impotent rage. To rub a pinch of salt into their wounded pride, he smiled and waved as if bidding close friends so long. Then he trotted to the open slope and descended to verdant woodland. His prospects were looking up. He had a horse and two weapons. And unless the Crows were as good at tracking as Apaches, he would soon give them the slip.

To that end, Nate spent the time until sunset riding a zigzag pattern through the thickest brush and over the hardest ground he could find. Periodically he dismounted and used small branches to wipe out his tracks, then sprinkled leaves and bits of grass on the marks the branches made.

As the sun set in the west, Nate halted beside a ribbon of a creek. He allowed the weary horse to drink, tied it to a brush, and climbed a nearby tall pine. From 80 feet above the ground he enjoyed a panoramic view of the countryside. Nowhere were there any Crows.

Safe at last, Nate collected two old bird nests on the way down and used them as kindling for his small fire. He had to go without food, but a grumbling stomach seemed such a paltry problem after the ordeal he had just been through. He only hoped his mentor and the greenhorn were faring half as well.

At that very moment, Shakespeare McNair lay on his left side near a crackling fire, his arms and legs tied tight. He shifted a few inches to glance at the man from Maine, and remarked, "Why so downcast, my young friend? You're still alive, and where there's life, there's hope."

Tim Curry had been staring sadly at the dancing flames. He looked at the mountain man and said bitterly, "Please, McNair. There's no need for you to treat me like a child. I might be new to these mountains, but I'm not an idiot. I know we'll be killed as soon as we reach the Crow village."

Shakespeare made a clucking sound, then quoted, "He does nothing but frown. As who should say, 'if you will not have me, choose.' He hears merry tales and smiles not. I fear he will prove the weeping philosopher when he grows old, being so full of unmannerly sadness in his youth."

"How can you prattle on so?" Tim snapped. "Your silly words do nothing but make me feel worse than I already do."

"It's human nature, son, to be as happy as we make up our minds to be."

Tim snorted. "No sane man could be happy at a time like this. We're staring death in the face and you want to make merry!" He shook his head in disgust. "My parents were right. I never should have left Maine."

Shakespeare saw no point in trying to cheer the greenhorn. He arched his back so he could see the Crows, who were clustered together across the fire. They were a quiet, gloomy bunch, no doubt because of the death of the warrior killed by Nate. The body had been brought back and draped in blankets, and now lay over by the trees, as far from the horses as possible.

Just then Whirlwind Hawk rose and walked over. "I have decided we will all go on to our village tomorrow instead of spending more time searching for your friend. Invincible One can send warriors to look for him, if he chooses."

"You will never find Grizzly Killer," Shakespeare predicted. "He is not about to let himself be caught a second time. He seldom makes the same mistake twice."

"We will see." Whirlwind Hawk squatted. "Your friend is very clever. I will admit that much. It took great skill to elude Stalking Fox and the others."

Shakespeare rolled onto his back so he could look at the warrior without having to bend his neck. "Even as we speak, Grizzly Killer is on his way to the camp of the Blanket Chief. Every trapper in the region will be after you before too long. You would be wise to let us go before there is more bloodshed."

"Let them come. Invincible One fears no man, not even the Blanket Chief."

"This chief of yours must be very brave."

"His medicine is the greatest of all. No one can kill him."

McNair wasn't sure if he had heard correctly. "Everyone dies."

"Not him," Whirlwind Hawk repeated. "When he first came among us, some doubted. He agreed to be tested, and let men stab him and shoot him with arrows and guns. One even tried to pierce him with a lance. Nothing hurt him. So he was named the Invincible One because his body is as hard as iron."

"How can any man have a body made of iron?" Shakespeare responded skeptically.

"I did not say it is made of iron," the Crow corrected him. "It is *like* iron."

"The meaning is the same. Unless you speak in riddles."

"If you knew what I know, you would not think so," Whirlwind Hawk said. "Soon all will be made clear. Invincible One will decide what to do with you and the young one. If he does as he has done with the others—" The warrior did not finish the statement.

"What others?" Shakespeare prompted. "Have you taken more trappers prisoner?"

"Invincible One will answer all your questions."

Shakespeare was getting nowhere with the direct approach, so he tried to learn more by saying, "This Invincible One of yours is going to bring a lot of misery down on the Crows if he makes war on the Blanket Chief. Just ask the Blackfeet and the Piegans. They have been trying to defeat him for years."

"Your threats are empty," Whirlwind Hawk said, but his tone lacked conviction.

"Keep on believing that and lives will be lost on both sides," Shakespeare said, continuing to bluff. "And once the whites know the truth about your people, there will be no more trade between us. The friendly tribes will get guns and blankets and steel knives, but not the Crows."

Again McNair had struck a nerve. Whirlwind Hawk was most displeased. "Without guns and steel knives we will not be able to fend off the attacks of our enemies. Already the Blackfeet and their allies have many more guns than we do. If they obtain more, my people might be driven from our land."

"Just as they once drove the Snakes off to take this territory," Shakespeare said. "Perhaps your people will be able to find new land to the west. I hear there is plenty of desert no one claims as their own."

"You would be wise not to mock us, Wolverine." So saying, the warrior rose and walked stiffly off.

Shakespeare chuckled while making himself as comfortable as possible. His wrists ached abominably and his feet were practically numb, but neither bothered him much. They couldn't hold a candle to the terrible wounds he'd once sustained during a trip to the Mandan country when a grizzly had about ripped him apart. He'd survived that; he'd survive this.

"McNair?" Tim Curry unexpectedly whispered.

"What?"

"I just had a thought."

"Thinking is a good habit to get into."

"Do you reckon King will try to rescue us?"

"As sure as I'm lying here."

"Tonight?"

"There's no telling. He'll make his move when he figures he has the best chance. Whatever you do, don't give him away if you should see him snaking up on us to cut us loose."

"I'd never do that. What do you take me for?"

Shakespeare merely smiled and lay back to rest. There were times when keeping one's mouth shut was wisest. Curry was miserable enough without being told he didn't appear to have the temperament necessary to be a successful trapper, that perhaps he should go on back to Maine and take up clerking for a living.

The thought gave Shakespeare pause. Who was he to judge others? So what if the young man was headstrong, rash, and moody? Shakespeare well remembered another young man with a similar disposition who had gone on to become a first-rate mountaineer. He had to extend the benefit of the doubt until Curry was able to prove himself, one way or the other.

Closing his eyes, Shakespeare allowed himself to drift asleep. He entertained no fear of having his throat slit in the middle of the night. The Crows wanted them alive, for the time being, at least. And he'd need his wits sharp on the morrow, especially if they reached the village and he met the mysterious Invincible One face to face.

But as things turned out, the journey to the Crow village required four days of hard riding. Whirlwind Hawk refused to say exactly when they'd arrive, so Shakespeare was as surprised as Tim Curry when they surmounted a rise and saw spread out below them scores of painted lodges. The village was nestled in a verdant valley, southwest of a small lake. Hundreds of horses were in evidence, along with yapping dogs, playing children, and too many women and warriors to count.

"The Lord preserve us!" Tim Curry blurted out. It was the first Indian village he had ever seen, and while he was impressed by its orderly arrangement, and even impressed by its picturesque beauty, he was filled with dawning horror at the thought that soon, very soon, he would be slain in the most gruesome manner conceivable.

Shakespeare saw the younger man's expression and advised, "Don't show that you're afraid, Troilus. Indians don't respect a man who is yellow. They'll grant a brave man a quick death. But cowards they torture just to hear them squeal."

"I won't let on," Tim said, and swallowed hard. For the life of him he couldn't understand how McNair could be so calm.

Sentries alerted the encampment to the arrival of the search party, and by the time Whirlwind Hawk guided his party in among the lodges a considerable body of curious Crows had gathered. Shakespeare rode straight and tall, smiling at the children and women and nodding respectfully at warriors, particularly the older warriors. He hoped there were some who would know him and speak on his behalf at the tribal council that would decide their fate.

Shakespeare was mildly puzzled when they were taken to a small lodge instead of to the large lodge of the chief, conspicuous by its location and size. He offered no protest when several strapping warriors hauled him from his horse and rather roughly shoved him inside. He quickly moved aside, and moments later young Curry stumbled through the entrance and collapsed in the very spot he had vacated.

"What now?" Tim asked.

"I reckon we sit and wait."

"That's all?"

"Unless you'd rather sing. Do you know the words to 'Rock of Ages'?"

"You *are* insane, McNair. Joking? *Now?*"

"There's a method to my madness," Shakespeare replied. "When they hear us singing they'll think we don't have a care in the world. It will show them we're brave men deserving of fair treatment."

"I can't."

"Try."

"Maybe later," Tim said. He saw Crows filing past the opening to peer in at them. "Damn," he muttered. "They're acting as if we're on exhibit."

"In a sense we are," Shakespeare said. "It isn't every day they see white men. The same thing would happen if you were to take five or six of them for a stroll through New York City."

"That's different. They're savages."

Shakespeare sat up and frowned. "Son, if you

truly believe that, then you're worse off than I thought. Indians are people like you and me. No more, no less. There are good and bad, kind and wicked, rich and poor. They live, eat, make love, and die much as we do. They're allotted this earth for the same one brief lifetime, and are as scared of the veil as we are."

"How can you say we're the same? They scalp whites, for God's sake."

"And whites scalp them for money's sake."

"They live in the wild in a primitive state."

"Does living in cities and towns, cramped up like too many prairie dogs in a colony, make us smarter or better than they are? As for being primitive, since when is living in harmony with Nature a crime? Isn't that what Adam and Eve did before they were cast out of the Garden?"

"You make them sound better than our own kind," Tim said testily. "Maybe that comes from having lived among them so long."

"I'm not saying any such thing," Shakespeare said. "I'm just trying to get the point across that we don't have a right to brand them as savages when we're not all that refined ourselves."

"You can talk until you're blue in the face but you'll never convince me," Tim declared. "Maybe some of them are good. It hardly matters. Because they're all heathens, every last mother's son of them."

Shakespeare lapsed into silence. It would be a study in futility to try and make the greenhorn understand. Some of life's lesson had to be learned through experience. He was toying with the idea of taking a nap when outside the lodge a commotion broke out. A shadow darkened the opening, and a Crow warrior with high cheekbones and a cleft chin poked his head in.

"One of you speaks our tongue, I am told."

"I do," Shakespeare confessed. "Are you Invincible One, the chief?"

For a few fleeting moments the warrior's features underwent a startling change, reflecting intense, bitter hatred. He seemed to wrestle with inner demons, then composed himself and said, "I am a chief, but I am Two Humps."

"The father of Gray Badger."

Two Humps entered and squatted in front of McNair. "Then it is true," he said anxiously. "You have seen him. How is he?"

"Fine, the last I saw," Shakespeare answered. "He was half starved when we found him so we gave him some food. I tried to find out why he was all by himself, but before he could tell me anything we were interrupted by Whirlwind Hawk." Shakespeare paused. "I got the idea he had run away from your village. He was afraid we would bring him back."

"Afraid?"

"He claimed he would be beaten."

A cloud flitted across the warrior's face and he clenched his fists until the knuckles were white. "I do not beat my children," he said harshly.

Shakespeare believed him. The raw emotion the father showed was genuine. "Your son told me that Invincible One would order him to be beaten."

Two Humps glanced darkly at the entrance. "I would die before I would let him go so far," he said half to himself. "There are limits."

"I do not understand," Shakespeare said kindly, hoping to elicit more information. "Since when do chiefs have the right to order a boy whipped? I lived among your people once, and I never heard of such a thing."

The warrior glowered, but not at McNair. "There have been many changes in our village since the Invincible One came to live among us. Few of them have been for the better."

"Where did he come from? Another Crow village?"

"No," Two Humps said. "He is not a Crow."

The revelation shocked McNair. It was unthinkable for any tribe to accept as chief one who was not of their blood. The Invincible One's medicine had to be great indeed to have accomplished such a miracle. "How can this be?" he asked. "When I lived among you, a Crow had to prove himself worthy over many winters before he became a chief. He had to demonstrate his bravery by earning many coup, and show his generosity to his people by giving often to those in need. Has this outsider done all that?"

"He counted four coup when he led a raid on the Piegans to punish them for attacking us," Two Humps said.

"Four? That is all? Most chiefs I know have counted twenty or thirty."

"And he does pass out coffee and sugar and blankets to those in need."

"How does he get them? Trading with whites?"

The Crow appeared reluctant to discuss the issue. After a bit he said, "It is not wise to question the Invincible One's actions. Since no one can kill him, he can do as he pleases."

"Including beating a small boy if he wants?" Shakespeare asked.

Two Humps abruptly stood. "I thank you, white man, for being kind to my son. If the decision were mine to make, I would restore all of your belongings and allow you to go your way in peace, as a friend. But Invincible One has other plans for you. There is nothing I can do." Stooping, he went out.

The interview had left Shakespeare more confused than ever. He wished he had thought to inquire about which tribe the Invincible One hailed from. He moved to the opening, expecting to find the Crows had begun to disperse. To his consternation, he saw the warriors huddled to one side while the women and children waited in an expectant group as if for an important decision.

"What's happening?" Tim asked.

"I'm not sure."

"What did that warrior want?"

"He was the boy's father," Shakespeare said absently. He was more interested in the tall figure at the center of the knot of warriors, a figure to whom all the others were listening. It had to be the Invincible One. Shakespeare shifted, trying to get a better glimpse, but too many Crows blocked his view.

"Listen, I've been thinking again," Tim said. "What if we try to buy our freedom? We'll offer them five rifles for each of us in exchange for letting us go."

"We don't have ten rifles."

"So we'll pretend we can get our hands on them. We'll tell the Crows that if they'll take us to Fort William, the guns will be theirs. As highly as they value firearms, they're bound to go for the deal. And once we're there, we're safe."

"It won't work. They wouldn't trust us."

"Where's the harm in trying?"

"Once the Crows learn we've tricked them, there will be one hell of a fight. A lot of good men would die on our account." Shakespeare glanced at the greenhorn. "I for one wouldn't want their deaths on my conscience."

"You'd rather be killed?"

Amazement froze the reply on Shakespeare's lips. The clustered warriors had suddenly parted, revealing the tall figure in the middle. The man strode in lordly fashion toward the lodge, the warriors following like dutiful children.

It had to be the Invincible One.

And he was white!

Chapter Six

About the time that Shakespeare McNair was making the shocking discovery that would shortly embroil him in a desperate fight for his life, Nate King was nearing the Crow village from the southwest. He spied a rise ahead, and stopped in the shelter of a pine in case the war party had stopped on the crest to scour the area for enemies. After making certain there were no silhouettes on the skyline, he started around the tree, then drew up in alarm and dropped his hand to his knife.

Voices carried on the breeze, mingled with low laughter. Nate had to lean forward to see through the woods to his left. A pair of Crow warriors were 40 yards off, moving parallel with the trail he followed. One had a dead buck hanging over the back of his mount. Judging by the noise they were making, neither had any idea there was anyone else close by.

Nate smiled. For the warriors to be so relaxed and noisy indicated they were close to their village. He observed them climb the rise and disappear beyond. Then, hugging all available cover, he rode to the top himself.

From behind a row of pines Nate gazed down on the Crow village. The entire populace was gathered near a small lodge, where quite a tumult was taking place. The press of people prevented him from learning the exact cause, but the racket did not bode well for McNair and Curry.

Wheeling the horse, Nate rode to the bottom of the hill and slanted to the west. He intended to circle around until he could locate his friends. As he drew abreast of a small stand of shimmering aspens, the horse glanced into the stand and whinnied.

Nate looked but didn't see anything. He rode on, passed the aspens, and trotted toward high brush. A low growl snapped him around, and this time he saw a village mongrel bristling in feral anger while behind it stood three small boys armed with small bows. They gaped in astonishment at him. Then one gave a shout and the trio pivoted on their heels and fled through the aspens with their dog at their heels.

Instantly Nate turned into the forest and galloped westward away from the village. The boys would spread the alarm and within minutes there would be anywhere from 50 to 100 warriors spreading out across the countryside after him. He went over two miles, then climbed a switchback to an upland bench. There he halted to rest his mount and ascertain if the Crows were tracking him.

There wasn't much daylight left. The lengthening shadows plunged the lower slopes in gloom. Nate surveyed them without result. He feared greatly for the safety of the others, but was not about to do anything rash. If he was caught, the others had no hope at all.

In due course the sun sank. The Crows never appeared. Nate became restless and paced back and forth, unable to explain their absence. He had been in such a hurry to escape he hadn't bothered to hide his tracks, so they should have had no trouble sticking to his trail. Either they hadn't been interested in catching him, which he didn't believe for a minute, or else the boys hadn't told anyone they'd seen him, which seemed highly unlikely. Whatever, he was not going to delay any longer.

Picking his way carefully, Nate threaded a roundabout route through the woodland. The bench fell far behind, and he presently saw pinpoints of light in the distance. Since he had the wind at his back and didn't care to have the dogs detect his scent, he angled to the south, then eastward. Approximately a quarter of a mile from the encampment, he halted and secured his horse to an oak tree.

Holding the butcher knife in one hand, the tomahawk in the other, Nate crept forward, stopping repeatedly to listen. The village was quieter than it should be. Absent were the night singers, the beat of drums, the muted drone of voices. He advanced until he could see individual lodges, then flattened and crawled. All the dwellings were lit from within, and in addition a few outside fires blazed. The latter might give him away should the light reflect off his pale skin at the wrong moment, so he paused to smear dirt on his cheeks, brow, and chin.

Snaking into a thicket, Nate stalked to the very perimeter of the village. He saw horses behind every lodge, but not nearly as many as there should be. And suddenly the odd lack of activity made sense. Most of the warriors were gone.

Nate was thoroughly mystified. Where had the Crow men gone, if not after him? What else could have drawn them all from the village? An enemy war party perhaps, or a report by a scout of a big group of trappers nearby. Yet he had seen no sign of either.

He decided not to look a gift horse in the mouth. With the majority of warriors gone, his task was less dangerous but far from a cinch. The lodge he must reach stood 60 yards off. In between were 14 other lodges, and there was no cover whatsoever.

Boldly rising, Nate tucked his weapons under his belt and entered the Crow village. He strolled along as if he didn't have a care in the world, prudently holding his head low so his features were in shadow. From a distance he might be mistaken for a Crow, but a close scrutiny would give him away. Above all else he must hide his beard.

Nate passed the first three lodges without mishap. In each people talked softly. There was no yelling in a village at night, none of the rowdy noise one associated with certain establishments in towns and cities. Neighbors were respectful of one another, and violators were subject to being disciplined by the tribal police, members of a warrior society appointed for just such a purpose.

The fourth lodge reared before him. Nate swung wide so as not pass too close to the entrance, and as he did the flap parted and out came an elderly woman supporting herself with a cane. She glanced at him and he quickly looked away, but gave a little wave and went on, hardly daring to breathe until he had gone far enough to justify safely looking over his shoulder. The woman had trudged to another teepee and was just entering.

Nate congratulated himself on his narrow escape and quickened his pace. He went by two more

lodges, and was halfway to the sixth when a
bulky shape detached itself from the side of the
teepee and came straight toward him. In a flash
he guessed the truth. As was customary with many
tribes, two unwed lovers were taking a stroll with a
buffalo robe thrown over their shoulders. Kneeling,
he fiddled with his left moccasin, pretending to be
adjusting the binding. Out of the corner of his eye
he saw the pair come closer, ever closer. Then they
were a yard away and he heard a soft giggle and the
tinkle of a tiny bell. Raising a hand to his chin as if
scratching it, he risked a look, and had to check an
impulse to exhale in relief when the lovers went on
into the night without so much as acknowledging
his presence.

Nate hastened on. The small lodge was the only
dark dwelling in the camp. He half expected to
find guards, but there were none. Drawing his
knife and holding it next to his right leg, he
walked to the entrance and sank to one knee.
The flap was tied up. With a sinking feeling in his
gut, he slid inside. "Shakespeare?" he whispered.
"Curry?"

The total blackness took a few seconds for Nate's
eyes to penetrate, and when they had, he under-
stood why he received no reply. The lodge was
empty. At a loss to know what to do next, Nate
turned and scanned the village. He had no idea
whether his friends were already dead or whether
they had been moved to another lodge. The only
thing he did know was that he couldn't very well
go from teepee to teepee searching for them.

Nate moved to the opening to leave, but stopped
when he saw an inky form walking toward him.
He darted to one side to wait for the Crow to
pass. Moccasins crunched on the dry earth, drawing nearer. To his dismay, they halted in front of

the lodge and a warrior spoke, apparently address-
ing him. With a start he realized the Crow had gotten a glimpse of him and mistaken him for another
warrior. No doubt the man wanted to know why
he was in there.

The Crow spoke again, more insistently. Nate
clasped the knife hilt firmly and grunted an inarticulate answer. He heard the rustle of buckskin.
The black outline of a human head and neck poked
into the interior. The Crow said a single word. Then
Nate pounced. He grabbed the warrior's hair and
yanked, hauling the man inside even as he drove
the keen blade into the Crow's throat. The warrior
stumbled to his knees, wheezing horribly as blood
gushed from his severed jugular. Nate stabbed
again, sinking the knife in the Crow's chest. The
man grabbed Nate's arm and tried to pry it loose
while simultaneously opening his mouth to shout
or scream.

Nate slammed the Crow to the bare earth and
leaped on the man's back to keep him pinned
down. The Crow gurgled, thrashed, and flailed in
a frenzied effort to shake Nate off and stand. Slowly
but surely his movements weakened, then subsided
altogether. Nate stayed on top another minute for
good measure.

A peek outside verified no one had heard the
scuffle. Nate ran his hands over the warrior's waist
and found another knife and a small pouch. Both
he appropriated. After dragging the corpse to the
back of the teepee, he cautiously stepped outside.
Rather than walk all the way around the lodge circle, Nate opted to make a beeline and cut across
the open middle space. Tucking his chin to his
chest, he hastened off. Somewhere close a dog
barked, making him jump. He looked, saw no sign
of it, and walked briskly on.

Nate was halfway to the other side when he saw a couple under a buffalo robe. It must be the same pair he'd seen earlier, he thought. They were bundled in the hairy folds, their heavy breathing clearly audible. Nate intended to give them a wide berth. But as he swung to the right to go around them, the robe unexpectedly fell to their shoulders. Before he could avert his face, the pretty young woman saw him.

Nate was on them as the woman's scream blasted his eardrums. The young warrior twisted. The robe bulged as he moved his arms to grab a weapon. Nate slugged him full on the jaw, then spun and raced for the trees. On all sides there were shouts and Crows spilled from every lodge, seeking the source of the disturbance. Most were women.

Nate was about to pass between the two teepees nearest the thicket when someone spotted him and had to let the whole village know. To his right were tethered war horses, some grazing, unfazed by the uproar. He swerved and jumped onto the back of a chestnut.

A sleek warrior carrying a war club sped around one of the lodges and launched himself at Nate as Nate wheeled the horse. The club arced at Nate's head and Nate jerked aside and kicked, dumping the warrior on his backside. Poking his heels into the chestnut, Nate galloped into the forest and fled for his life.

The din being raised by the Crows was loud enough to be heard for miles. Nate didn't know if any would give chase but he was taking no chances. He pushed the chestnut despite the ever-present peril of the horse stepping into a rut or animal burrow and suffering a broken leg.

Nate was greatly upset by the outcome of his rescue attempt. He had lost the element of surprise. If the Crows still had McNair and Curry, they would take steps to ensure another such try was thwarted. His prospects of saving them would vanish completely.

On into the wilderness Nate rode for over 15 minutes. He had not been paying much attention to his direction of travel, and reined up to get his bearings. From the position of the North Star he knew he was riding due east. The forest had gone completely silent, and in that silence he couldn't miss hearing the drumming of hooves hundreds of feet to the rear.

It was hard to tell how many there were. Nate galloped to the southeast, pleased when the woods ended and a lowland plain stretched out before him. He flew through high grass, the wind whipping his long hair, on the lookout for roving beasts. Panthers, grizzlies, and wolves were partial to hunting their prey at night, and the last thing he needed was to stumble on one of them with the Crows breathing hot and heavy down his neck. Yet that was exactly what happened.

Nate came to a rocky knoll and angled to the left to pass it. He saw a large animal rear up on the slope. A rumbling snarl identified the creature, and with the speed of thought it gave chase. The chestnut didn't seem to fully appreciate the danger until a paw the size of a melon took a swipe at its tail. Fear lent renewed vigor to its limbs.

Nate glanced over a shoulder and saw the gaping jaws and glistening teeth of the grizzly. It wasn't as big as the one in the valley, a small consolation given that it was nearly the size of the chestnut and could disembowel the horse in an instant if

it caught up. Nate would have given anything for
a loaded flintlock.

Full-grown bears were capable of astonishing
speeds that belied their immense size. They rivaled
horses over short distances but lacked endurance.
This one was typical of the breed, and for ten
harrowing seconds Nate thought he would be torn
from the chestnut's back and ripped to pieces on
the dank earth. The bear's fetid breath filled his
nostrils as its claws shortened the chestnut's tail
even further.

Then the horse pulled ahead. A growl of bestial fury was the grizzly's reaction, and it stopped.
Nate made no attempt to slow his mount until they
had gone over half a mile. At a walk he rode to
the top of a hill. From there he could see clear to
the village. He thought he had shaken the Crows,
but he was wrong. A lone warrior was two hundred yards off, paralleling the course he had tak-
en.

Nate was impressed by the brave's skill. Most
men would have lost track of him long before this.
He trotted down the hill and into a tract of forest
to make it difficult for the Crow to use a rifle or
bow. He also sought a spot to ambush his pursuer.
No favorable sites presented themselves, and in a
short while the trees ended.

Nate went 15 feet out and drew rein. Sliding
down, he left the chestnut standing there and
sprinted back to the forest. A young spruce tree
afforded him the hiding place he needed. He drew
one of the hunting knives, then pressed an ear to
the ground. The dull thud of hooves indicated the
Crow was a lot closer.

Practically hugging the spruce, Nate crouched
and held the knife poised to strike. He figured the
rider would emerge about ten feet to his right. He

could see the pale horse but the warrior was hidden in shadow. Suddenly, as if suspecting a trap, the Crow stopped.

Nate's skin prickled. He wondered if the warrior could see him, if there was a rifle being trained on him or a bow being drawn back. Then the Crow approached slowly. Nate lowered himself until his chin brushed the grass. The horse's head hove into sight. Nate could see its legs but not much of the man astride it. Again the Crow halted and Nate knew the warrior was staring at the chestnut.

In a lithe motion Nate surged erect and sprang. He had taken two steps and was in midair when he saw that he had erred. The rider wasn't a man after all. Unable to stop, Nate caught the boy around the waist, propelling both of them into the weeds. He managed to land on his shoulder and absorbed the brunt of the impact. Rolling, he released his hold and rose partway.

Gray Badger was shaken but unhurt. He stood, his posture suggesting he would flee at any more sudden movements.

Nate wedged the knife under his belt and employed sign. "I am sorry, son of Two Humps. I thought you were a warrior come to kill me. Are you hurt?"

The boy sniffed as if insulted. "Crow men are not weaklings." He nodded at the chestnut. "That was a fine trick, Grizzly Killer. I must remember it when I go on the war path."

Standing, Nate gazed westward. "Are you alone?"

"Yes. I have been following you ever since you were captured by Whirlwind Hawk."

Gray Badger walked to his horse, which Nate now recognized as one of the pack animals belonging to Tim Curry. In all the confusion back in the valley, Nate had never noticed it was missing from the string. Understandable, given his predicament.

"I slipped off during the fight," the boy confirmed. "No one saw me go, and I hid on the other side of the stream until they gave up looking for me. Then I trailed them, keeping far back. Much later I saw that you had broken away and were also trailing them, but I could not catch up to you before you reached the village."

"You were spying on the village and saw me leave?" Nate signed.

"Yes. My horse is not as fast as yours or I would have been with you sooner." Gray Badger gave the animal a light whack on the side. "I am glad you were the one the bear tried to eat and not me. It would have caught me easily. When I heard it chase you, I went far around."

"You are brave beyond your years," Nate signed, and meant every word. It took courage for anyone to brave the wilderness alone. For someone of the boy's tender years to dare the feat was rare. Gray Badger's pluck reminded Nate of his own son, Zach, and he almost reached out and tousled the boy's hair.

"Question. Did you find your friends?" Gray Badger asked.

"No," Nate signed, the reminder kindling anew his anxiety over his mentor's plight. "I have no idea where they are. Do you?"

"I did not get too close to the village," the boy signed. "The Invincible One might see me."

Nate brought the chestnut over and moved under the overspreading limbs of a tall fir. Sitting with his back to the trunk, he watched the young Crow tie the packhorse, then signed, "Would this Invincible One have my friends killed?"

"He kills all whites," Gray Badger answered, and added hastily, "Many of my people want him to stop but they are afraid of him, afraid of his powerful medicine." He paused. "How do you fight someone who can not be killed?"

Believing the boy was exaggerating, Nate inquired, "Has anyone tried?"

"Eight warriors so far. I saw one of them try. His name was Black Shield, and he had counted eighteen coup. He challenged Invincible One in front of everyone, then shot an arrow into Invincible One's chest."

"What happened?" Nate asked when the boy fell silent.

"I could not believe my eyes," Gray Badger signed slowly. "The arrow hit Invincible One but bounced off. He laughed, as he often does when he hurts others, and he shot Black Shield through the head. No one has dared go up against his medicine since."

Nate did not know what to make of the story. He'd expect such an outrageous tale from a half-drunk trapper, but the boy was sincere. Maybe, he reasoned, he could get at the truth another way. He knew that the Crows, like other tribes, had a strong belief in talismans, as the trappers called them, everyday articles believed to bestow good medicine on those fortunate enough to possess them. It might be something as simple as an eagle claw, or a piece of wood, or a stone or a seed. Whatever, it would be wrapped in a piece of skin and worn touching the owner's body so that the power of the charm was most potent. "What gives Invincible One his great medicine?" he asked.

"No one knows."

"Has he always been invincible?"

Gray Badger yawned. "We have not been told. He will not talk about his power with anyone."

Nate felt an urge to yawn himself and fought it off. "How many whites has he killed?"

"Nine or ten, I think." The boy lay on his side. "It might be more. I cannot remember. I am too tired."

Nate wanted to learn more, but it was evident the little Crow was exhausted. For that matter, so was he. He'd slept fitfully at best the past few days. "Tomorrow I must try to find my friends. Will you help me?"

"I will do what I can," Gray Badger signed wearily.

"Perhaps your father would aid us."

The boy's eyes shot wide and he swiveled to glare at Nate. "Do not think such a thing. He would be in too much danger. Invincible One would be very mad if he found out and might harm him."

Nate smiled. "So you do care for him."

"Of course I do."

"Then why did you run away?"

"I had to. I made Invincible One angry."

"How?"

"I would rather not say," Gray Badger signed, then tried to make himself comfortable.

"What harm can it do?" Nate pressed.

Gray Badger pondered a few moments. "Very well. I was curious, like all the boys. I wanted to learn where Invincible One gets his medicine. So when Lame Elk, my friend, dared me, I spied on Invincible One by cutting a hole in the side of his lodge."

"And he caught you?"

"Yes, and came running out, very mad. I shamed myself by running. He yelled for men to catch me so he could beat me. Since there are some who do whatever he asks, and since I knew they would have to fight my father to get to me, I left."

More pieces of the puzzle fit into place. Nate was more impressed than ever by the boy's maturity.

"You left to protect your father. You did not want him clashing with Invincible One."

"What else could I do?" Gray Badger lay flat. "Now excuse me. I must sleep."

In under a minute the young Crow was lost to the world. Nate tried to stay awake a while longer to mull over the best course of action for him to take, but he was unable to keep his eyes open. It seemed as if he had hardly closed them when chirping sparrows brought him around to find the sun peeking over the horizon. Nate stretched as he stood.

Gray Badger slept on undisturbed. The pack-horse was trying to get at a patch of nearby grass. But there was no sign of the chestnut, which had wandered off during the night.

Nate had a good idea where the animal had gotten to, but before looking he untied the packhorse so it could get at the grass. A short run brought him to the narrow plain. His hunch proved accurate, for 40 yards out grazed the chestnut. Nate started to fetch it, then froze.

A quarter of a mile beyond the horse a large body of Crows had appeared, evidently all the warriors missing from the village the night before. And they were heading right toward him.

Chapter Seven

Shakespeare McNair's astonishment at discovering the Invincible One to be white was compounded by a second shock when the man came close enough for Shakespeare to see his features. "Well, I'll be damned!" he exclaimed.

"What's the matter?" Tim Curry asked, moving closer.

"Why, he is the prince's jester," Shakespeare quoted. "A very dull fool."

Tim peered out and blinked several times. "As I live and breathe, we're saved! That trapper must be friendly with the Crows! I bet they'll let us go if he asks them."

"I'd take that bet but I'd be stealing your money," Shakespeare said. He moved aside as the Invincible One bent to enter. He studied the man's harshly angular features, and saw recognition in the other's darkly smoldering eyes. "Fancy meeting you again," he commented.

99

Jacob Pierce knelt in the opening and gave them both a look of utter disdain before focusing on Shakespeare. "Greetings, McNair. I never figured you would be careless enough to be taken by the Crows or anyone else. Must be your years catching up with you."

Tim Curry was so overjoyed to see a fellow trapper that he didn't notice the man's expression or tone. He leaned forward and twisted to reveal his bound wrists, declaring, "I don't know who you are, friend, but I'll be eternally grateful if you would cut us loose and convince these savages to release us. You have no idea of the nightmare we've been through. Until I saw you, I thought we were doomed."

Pierce reached out and touched the rope. Without warning, he gripped Curry's forearms and gave them a brutal wrench, causing the greenhorn to cry out. Curry tried to pull loose but couldn't. "Who is this fool, McNair?" Pierce sneered, and shoved Curry to the ground.

"Allow me to introduce young Troilus," Shakespeare responded. "His heart is in the right place but he left his mind back in Maine."

"Troilus?" Pierce repeated, then frowned. "Oh. More of your nonsense. Well, the coons at the next Rendezvous will be spared from having to listen to your silliness."

"You've gone that far over the line, have you?"

"All the way and then some."

Tim Curry was rising to his knees, his cheek scraped from his fall. Complete confusion dominated him. He had no idea what to make of the cruel trapper's attitude and actions. "Why did you do that to me?" he demanded. "I haven't done you any wrong. We should be sticking together. The real enemies are the heathens."

Jacob Pierce laughed, a low, rumbling mockery of the greenhorn's remarks. "You're more of a jackass than I thought, hoss. Don't be fretting over the Crows. They're not the ones you have to worry about. *I* am."

"You?" Tim said in bewilderment. "But you're white, like us. Surely you don't want us to come to any harm."

"Just because someone has the same skin color as you doesn't make him your brother," Pierce said. "Out here in the wilderness it's every man for himself, boy. The stupid and the slow don't last long."

"I still don't understand. Why would you hurt us?" Tim asked. "Why would any sane man want to hurt another?"

"Bootle."

"What?"

"Come with me. I'll show you."

Shakespeare followed the other two out. The Crow women and children were gathered to the right, waiting expectantly. In front of the lodge two dozen warriors had arranged themselves in two long parallel rows about eight feet apart, each man holding a war club or tomahawk or knife. At sight of them, Shakespeare involuntarily tensed. "Damn you, Pierce," he said.

The Invincible One only chuckled. "As last words go, they're not very original." He walked to the next teepee, a larger dwelling, and opened the flap. "Take a gander, Troilus," he told the greenhorn, "and maybe then you can go to your grave knowing why you have to die."

Curry tentatively stepped to the opening. Inside were stacked bales of beaver fur, a fortune in plews nearly filling the bottom of the lodge. "My word," he blurted. "There must be hundreds!"

"Thousands," Jacob Pierce corrected. "A few more seasons and I'll be one of the richest men on the continent." He bent and touched one of the hides, stroking the fur as if caressing a lover. "A lot of hard work went into raising these plews, and not one lick of it was mine."

"Then how . . . ?" Tim began, and stopped, the awful implication hitting him with the force of a physical blow. "Sweet Jesus! You're killing trappers and stealing their catch!"

"At last! To think, I thought you were dumb!" Pierce put his hands on his hips and roared.

Shakespeare had taken all of the abuse he was going to tolerate. He squared his shoulders and announced, "If you're fixing to kill us, you turncoat son of a bitch, then do it. I'm sick of listening to you crow just to hear yourself flap your gums."

Pierce's humor vanished in a twinkling, to be replaced by scarlet wrath. "As you wish, McNair," he said gravely. "Although if I was in your shoes, I wouldn't be in such a hurry to meet my Maker." He motioned at the twin rows of stalwart warriors. "Have you ever seen a man run a gauntlet before? It's not a pretty sight. By the time you reach the end, if you live that long, you'll beg me to put you out of your misery."

"I've never groveled in my life," Shakespeare countered. "And as you pointed out, I'm too blamed old to start now." He wagged his arms. "Cut me loose and let's get cracking."

"McNair, no!" Tim butted in, aghast.

Shakespeare faced the greenhorn. "When a man's time comes, son, he has to meet it squarely, with all the gumption he can muster. Dying with dignity is one of the few graces afforded us, and I for one don't aim to pass up the chance to show I've learned more from life than not to sit downwind of men who have eaten beans for supper."

Pierce grinned. "And you had the gall to claim I like to hear myself talk! Have you ever listened to yourself, old-timer? At the Rendezvous you go on for hours reading that miserable book of yours aloud." He glanced at a third lodge, where all of the plunder the Crows had confiscated was stacked for his inspection. "Come to think of it, that damn book must be in one of your bags. It will make dandy kindling."

"You're lucky I don't have a gun," Shakespeare responded, "or I'd show these Crows that you're about as invincible as a bowl of mush."

"Am I indeed?" Pierce laughed, then gestured at a knot of warriors, among them Two Humps, who hurried to do his bidding. Seizing McNair and the greenhorn, the Crows hauled the pair to the end of the gauntlet. Both had their bounds removed, at which point the Crows formed a small ring around the two trappers and leveled rifles or drew knives.

"Just in case you get any crazy notions about trying to get away," Pierce said. He stood with his brawny arms folded, his brow knit, for half a minute. "It occurs to me, McNair, that I ought to demonstrate why the Crows gave me the name they did. You see, I once raised beaver in the same valley where Whirlwind Hawk found you. Then a war party trapped me, and I figured I was a goner for certain. But when they shot me, I wasn't hurt. Not so much as a scratch. That convinced them I was something special, so they brought me back for everyone else to see. Put me to the test, you might say."

"And you've had them wrapped around your finger ever since," Shakespeare said. "It must be a whopper of a trick you have up your sleeve."

"Oh, it's no trick," Pierce said. "You couldn't kill me if you wanted to."

"Care to let me prove you wrong?"

"Yes, as a matter of fact." Pierce unexpectedly drew one of the pistols at his waist. "But I'm not about to turn a gun over to a crafty bastard like you. Let's have your idiot friend show you I'm speaking with a straight tongue." He offered the flintlock to Curry. "Take this and shoot me."

The young man from Maine gaped at the piece, then at the madman who held it. Nothing in Tim's prior experience had ever prepared him for a situation so outlandish as this. He wished he was dreaming, wished he would wake up and find he had been slumbering in his own bed at his parents' home in Maine. "I've never killed anyone before," he said meekly.

"Then here's your chance," Pierce said, shoving the pistol at him. "Hell, everyone should kill somebody at least once just to know what it's like."

"You're insane."

Taking a short step, Jacob Pierce rammed the flintlock into the greenhorn's stomach. Tim Curry doubled over in excruciating torment and felt his stomach start to heave. Shakespeare moved to help, but a rifle muzzle blossomed in front of his nose.

"Now then, boy," Pierce said, grabbing Curry's chin. "You're going to do exactly as I say without any more of your guff or I'll have one of these Crows put a ball through your private parts. Savvy?"

Tim could scarcely breathe. He gulped in air, nodding briskly when Pierce raised the pistol to strike him again. "I'll do whatever you want," Tim said, and suddenly had a thought that electrified him into recovering swiftly. Pierce was the one responsible for killing and robbing trappers. Therefore, if he killed Pierce, the Crows might be willing to permit Shakespeare and him to depart unmolested. He listened to Pierce bark words at the Crows in their tongue.

"Take the gun," the murderer ordered.

Dutifully, Tim obeyed and put his thumb on the hammer.

"Don't cock it until I say," Pierce directed. "If you do, the Crows will make wolf meat of you." He backed up a half-dozen long paces, then held both arms out from his sides. "Now pull back the hammer."

Tim did.

"Aim at my heart."

Tim did, annoyed when his hand shook uncontrollably. He tried to steady his nerves through sheer force of will. Several of the Crows had trained rifles and bows on him, which didn't help his state of mind any.

"Come on, you dunderhead," Pierce taunted. "You can do it. Just think of me as your worst enemy."

Tim had no trouble in that regard. At length the shaking subsided and he took deliberate aim, centering the bead on the middle of the rogue's chest. Sweat broke out on his palm and his mouth abruptly went dry.

"When I count to five, squeeze the trigger."

Nodding once, Tim licked his lips and stilled the fluttering of his heart. He was so high-strung he nearly jumped when McNair spoke.

"What happens if he kills you, Pierce?"

"He won't."

"But what if he does?" Shakespeare said. "I want you to tell these Crows of yours to let us collect our fixings and leave if you go under."

"I hold all the cards here, McNair. Not you."

"Do you?" Shakespeare responded. "The only reason you want Troilus to shoot you is so you can prove to the Crows that not even other whites can kill you. This stunt is a big show you're putting on for their benefit. Survive, and they're liable to think you're all-powerful, a god in human form." Shakespeare took a step toward the greenhorn. "But if we don't do as you want, they might get the notion into their heads that you're not as high and mighty as you make yourself out to be. It might give a few an incentive to test your invincibility on their own."

"You always were a clever son of a bitch," Pierce said. "Too damn clever for your own good." He sighed. "All right. If I'm killed, you can go. My word on it."

"Tell them," Shakespeare said, and paid close attention as Pierce relayed the order. He was strongly tempted to make a grab for the flintlock in Curry's hand, but knew he'd be shot dead before he could. The greenhorn was pale, yet radiated a somber air of resolve. Shakespeare knew Curry would do it, and he had to admit that he was intensely curious to learn how Pierce pulled the chicanery off. Because it had to be deception of one kind or another. No man could live after being shot in the heart at such close range.

Pierce motioned impatiently. "Now can we get this over with? Shoot, boy, before I lose my temper and have the Crows separate you from your hair."

Tim closed his eyes for a moment and reached deep within himself for the spark of willpower needed to take the supreme step. He aimed again, then touched his finger to the trigger. Flame and smoke belched from the flintlock.

Jacob Pierce was flung backward, his arms flapping, to smack hard onto the ground. A great, collective gasp went up from the assembled Crows, and a number of warriors hastened toward him. They all stopped dead when Pierce abruptly sat up, a hand pressed to his chest, pain etching his features. He looked down at himself, at his bloodless hand, and smiled in personal triumph.

The greenhorn gawked, unable to accept the reality of the tableau.

And Shakespeare McNair so forgot himself as to snatch the empty pistol from Curry's grasp so he could sniff the barrel. There was no denying the gun had contained plenty of powder. "You didn't put in a ball," he guessed. "That's your secret, Pierce. You put in powder but no bullet."

"Think so, do you?" Pierce glanced at one of the warriors. "Let him load the pistol using your powder horn and ammo pouch. Keep a close eye on him. If he tries anything, kill him."

Shakespeare took the proffered items and set about reloading. First he added the right amount of powder. Too much, and the barrel would burst. Too little, and the bullet wouldn't penetrate. Then he wrapped the ball in a patch and tamped both down on top of the powder using a rod handed him by another Crow. When he was done he looked up and saw Jacob Pierce standing 15 feet away, waiting.

"I've heard tales about your marksmanship, McNair. They say you can shoot the eye out of a chipmunk at three hundred yards. Here's where you prove them right." Pierce slowly turned and spread his arms out. "Let's see if you can put one through my heart from the back. Put your shot smack between my shoulder blades."

Shakespeare straightened and cocked the flint-lock. He wanted nothing more than to put an end to Pierce's bloody spree, but he had never shot anyone in the back and wasn't inclined to start. "Turn around. I'd rather see your face when I pull the trigger."

"No, you'll do it through my back or not at all."

Everyone was watching intently. Shakespeare sighted halfway between Pierce's shoulders. In his mind's eye he envisioned the ball shattering the spinal column, ripping through Pierce's flesh into the heart, and exploding out the chest in a spray of blood and gore.

"I don't have all day."

Shakespeare hesitated. It went against his grain to shoot an unarmed man, no matter how vile the man might be. He had to remind himself of all the trappers Pierce had wiped out, all the innocent lives destroyed in the name of blatant greed. Then he stroked the trigger.

Jacob Pierce hurtled forward, stumbled to his knees, and collapsed. Shakespeare took a few steps, confident a spreading red strain would dampen the back of the renegade's shirt. To his consternation, no blood appeared. He saw Pierce twitch, then put both hands on the ground and push to his knees. Wearing a smile of pure evil, Pierce slowly turned.

"Nice shooting, McNair. If I was an ordinary man, I'd be gone beaver."

"Impossible," Shakespeare breathed. "I loaded the pistol myself."

"And you shot me yourself," Pierce bated him. "Maybe now you see why the Crows think I'm so special. They don't want to rile a man with medi-cine as strong as mine." He rose unsteadily, took a few deep breaths, then walked back. "Still, that packed quite a wallop. I hurt like hell."

Shakespeare stared at the flintlock in his hand. For the life of him he couldn't figure out how Pierce still lived. Could it be, he wondered, that the man actually *was* invincible? The very notion seemed preposterous, yet what other explanation was there? The next moment one of the warriors snatched the pistol from him and handed it to Pierce.

"I should thank you and the greenhorn, McNair. Now that the Crows have seen with their own eyes my medicine works on whites too, they'll be more agreeable to doing my bidding than ever before."

"And a lot more trappers will die," Shakespeare said bitterly.

"Another ten or twelve ought to give me enough plews to set myself up for life," Pierce boasted. He nodded at the plunder taken from McNair, King, and Curry. "The three of you hardly had any. I keep telling the damn Crows to only capture whites who have a lot of hides, but they can't seem to get it through their thick skulls. Twice now they've brought back trappers who hardly had a plew to their name." He tucked the spent pistol under his belt, beside another flintlock. "Now let's end this so I can get on to other things."

"End it?" Tim said, dread piercing him like a lance. For a while there he had forgotten all about the fate awaiting them. "You mean, kill us."

Pierce stepped to the gauntlet and bobbed his chin at the aisle between the rows of Crows. "Which one of you wants to go first? I can flip a coin if you can't make up your minds."

Tim glanced at the glittering knife in the bronzed hand of the first strapping warrior, and gulped. "What if we won't cooperate? What if we refuse to run?"

"Then I'll shoot you dead myself and have your bodies dumped in the woods for the coyotes and vultures to feast on," Pierce said.

Shakespeare boldly moved to the aisle and halted, his shoulder almost brushing Pierce. The warriors covering him likewise moved, two taking up positions on his right, the others behind Pierce. One of those on his right was Two Humps.

"I knew you'd be the noble sort and let the greenhorn go last," Pierce said sarcastically. "And to show you I can be just as noble, I'll grant a last request. Would you like a smoke? A chew? A cup of coffee?"

"I'd like a minute to make my peace with the Good Lord, if you don't mind," Shakespeare said.

Pierce's eyebrows arched. "I never took you for the religious type. Thought you had more sense than most." He shrugged. "If that's all you want, be my guest."

Folding his hands at his waist, Shakespeare bowed his head as if to pray and closed his eyes, but not all the way. Through cracked lids he watched those around him. He saw the Crows relax a bit, saw the pair with rifles lower the barrels a few inches. He saw Pierce shift to sneer at the greenhorn. And it was then, while they were all off guard, that he sprang into action, spinning and grabbing Pierce's second pistol before Pierce could think to stop him and whirling and shoving the cocked flintlock against Two Humps's temple before Two Humps or any of the other Crows could so much as move. "Lift a finger against us and he dies!" he shouted in their language.

A woman in the crowd screamed. Some of the warriors had started to lift their weapons and close in, but they halted on perceiving the consequences. They looked uncertainly at one another, and at the Invincible One.

Pierce had not batted an eye. Acting more amused than angry, he held out his hand. "Save us all some trouble. Give me the gun, McNair, and run the gauntlet."

"I'm not bluffing," Shakespeare bluffed.

"What do I care if you shoot him? He means nothing to me."

"But he means something to the Crows," Shakespeare said. "He's one of their chiefs, so he must have a lot of friends, a lot of influence. Let him die, and what will they think?"

Pierce's humor faded. "You keep trying to turn the tribe against me. Haven't you learned yet that I have them eating out of the palm of my hand?"

"Only so long as you keep them happy with fixings and baubles stolen from trappers. And only so long as they don't have to pay a high price in Crow blood." Shakespeare stepped behind Two Humps, who had not moved a muscle since being taken by surprise. The warrior held a knife, which Shakespeare plucked loose. "I want three horses brought over, Jacob. Then I want everyone to stand back or you'll have a heap of explaining to do as to why your medicine wasn't powerful enough to keep the chief from being killed."

"Damn you, McNair!"

"The horses. Now."

Pierce snapped commands and three mounts were promptly produced. Shakespeare had the greenhorn climb on first, then Two Humps. He moved the third animal, a stallion, next to the chief's horse and swung up while keeping the barrel pointed at his hostage. Many warriors fingered weapons but none proved foolhardy.

"We'll ride out slowly," Shakespeare said in both English and Crow. He walked the stallion alongside Two Humps until they were past the lodge circle. Looking back, he spied three boys talking to Pierce. Crow men were running every which way to fetch their war horses.

"What now?" Tim Curry asked.

"We ride like hell," Shakespeare said, and had Two Humps do just that, keeping pace beside him. They were a quarter of a mile from the encampment when a horde of wrathful Crows poured out in hot-blooded pursuit.

Join the Western Book Club and GET 4 FREE* BOOKS NOW!
A $19.96 VALUE!

Yes! I want to subscribe to the Western Book Club.

Please send me my **4 FREE* BOOKS**. I have enclosed
$2.00 for shipping/handling. Each month I'll receive the
four newest Leisure Western selections to preview for
10 days. If I decide to keep them, I will pay the Special
Members Only discounted price of just $3.36 each, a
total of $13.44, plus $2.00 shipping/handling ($19.50
US in Canada). This is a **SAVINGS OF AT LEAST
$6.00** off the bookstore price. There is no minimum
number of books I must buy, and I may cancel the pro-
gram at any time. In any case, the **4 FREE* BOOKS**
are mine to keep.

*In Canada, add $5.00 shipping/handling per order
for the first shipment. For all future shipments to
Canada, the cost of membership is $16.25 US,
which includes shipping and handling.
(All payments must be made in US dollars.)

NAME: _____

ADDRESS: _____

CITY: _____ STATE: _____

COUNTRY: _____ ZIP: _____

TELEPHONE: _____

E-MAIL: _____

SIGNATURE: _____

If under 18, Parent or Guardian must sign. Terms, prices, and conditions subject to change. Subscription subject
to acceptance. Dorchester Publishing reserves the right to reject any order or cancel any subscription.

Chapter Eight

Jacob Pierce was fit to be tied. Just when he thought he had proven to all the Crows that his medicine was greater than any man's, and shown the few remaining doubters among them that his invincibility was beyond question the genuine article, Shakespeare McNair had turned the tables and made him out to have no medicine at all and the brains of a turnip to boot. By getting the better of him, McNair had demonstrated that he could be beaten, and it might give some of the warriors who opposed him the wrong ideas.

So Pierce had one thing and one thing alone on his mind as he swept out of the village at the head of the ravening horde. He was going to kill the old mountain man in the most painful manner he could devise, and thereby show the Crows the fate of any who dared oppose him. By the time he was done, no warrior would dare think of crossing him.

Far to the east were the fleeing figures of
the three men. Pierce whipped his horse with
his reins and drove his heels into its flanks
to goad it to go faster. There were so many
Crows behind him, the combined thundering of
countless hoofs was almost deafening. He tried
not to think of the result should his mount trip
and go down before the unstoppable wave of
horseflesh.

And as if Pierce did not have enough to worry about, there was the report of the three boys
who had been out shooting birds with bows. They
claimed to have seen another white man in the
vicinity of the village, a white man who had ridden westward after encountering them. Pierce had
thanked them for the information, but had decided not to act on it until after the McNair affair
was settled. First things first, as the saying went.
Besides, a lone trapper was hardly cause for concern.

As time passed and Pierce realized he wasn't
gaining on his quarry, his anger steadily mounted.
He wanted to kick himself for not making the two
trappers run the gauntlet sooner. Had he not seen
fit to put on a grand performance for the Crows,
he wouldn't be in the fix he was in.

Presently the trio entered heavy woodland. Pierce
slowed when he came to the spot, and called for
the best trackers to come forward. Five warriors
were soon following the sign eastward as rapidly as
they could, but not rapidly enough to suit Pierce. It
soon became apparent McNair was as canny as an
old fox. The trail led through thorny thickets and
over the rockiest of ground, often doubling back
on itself. Time and again the whole party had to
sit and wait while the trackers scoured the ground
for prints.

Pierce chafed at the delays, but the thought of giving up and turning back never entered his head. He didn't dare, not until McNair and the greenhorn were stone-cold dead. If either escaped and spread word of his activities, every trapper in the Rockies would be after his skin. He wouldn't live out the month.

The sun gradually dipped ever lower in the blue vault of sky and hovered above the pink horizon. Pierce grew correspondingly more anxious as twilight approached. The Crows wouldn't ride at night, so unless McNair and company were caught soon, Pierce must resign himself to a fitful night spent sleeping on the ground and would have to resume the chase at first light. Neither prospect appealed to him.

Just when the outlook seemed bleakest, he had a lucky break.

A short while earlier, Shakespeare McNair had galloped down the slope of a ridge to the edge of a shelf. He fully expected to keep on going to the bottom of the low mountain he had crossed, but when he was yards shy of the rim he discovered to his chagrin that the shelf ended abruptly in a sheer drop-off over 60 feet high. At the bottom, buried in shadow, lay a murky lake.

"There's no way down!" Tim Curry wailed.

"We'll find one," Shakespeare said, reining to the right and trotting along the rim. Several small rocks rolled out from under his mount's hooves and plummeted over the precipice. So intent was he on locating a way of reaching the bottom that he didn't notice the Crow come up on his right side.

"Wolverine, there is a trail not far from here that will take you to the lake."

Shakespeare glanced at him. "Why tell me? You should want us dead after what I did."

Two Humps smiled. "A man who intends to shoot another man usually puts his finger on the trigger of his gun."

"Noticed, did you?"

"I wanted to be ready to jump aside if you started to shoot. The others were all watching you, not your hand." Two Humps paused. "You have great courage, white man. I hope you get away from the butcher who has led my people astray. Then they will see he is not as mighty as he claims."

A sudden thought made Shakespeare slow down. "Speaking of getting away, you have a son in need of your help. Swing wide of the village and head southwest until you reach the valley where your people first found Invincible One. Your boy should be somewhere in that area."

"You will permit me to ride off?"

"I will chase you off if you delay any longer."

The Crow's face betrayed baffled amazement, and something deeper. He leaned over to put a firm hand on McNair's shoulder. "From this moment on, we are brothers. Whatever I have is yours. You are welcome in my lodge any time, and your enemies are my enemies."

"Does that include Invincible One?"

Two Humps never hesitated. "It does. I have held my tongue long enough. After I find Gray Badger, I will appeal to my people to cast Invincible One out. He might be bullet-proof, but he can not stand up to all of us at once." He lowered his arm. "May the Great Spirit permit your moccasins to make tracks in many snows." With that, he tugged on his reins and galloped off into the timber.

Tim Curry was quick to draw abreast of McNair. "Why the devil did you let that heathen go? Now what will we do if Pierce catches us?"

"Fight."

The greenhorn muttered something.

"What was that, young Troilus?"

"My name is *Curry*," Tim snapped, "and I said that I'm sick and tired of all you crazy mountaineers. Each and every one of you doesn't care a whit whether you live or die."

"On the contrary, I wouldn't have all these white hairs if I wasn't extraordinarily fond of breathing," Shakespeare disagreed. "But when a man's back is to the wall, he has to give as good an account of himself as he can, not for posterity's sake, mind you, but on his own behalf."

"What the hell are you raving about now?"

"Dying, Tim."

"A gloomy subject, and one you talk about a lot."

"Only because out here dying is part and parcel of our lives each and every day," Shakespeare said. "Until you come to terms with how you're going to go out, you won't be able to deal with the wilderness on its own terms." He paused. "You came out here expecting paradise, and instead found that life in the raw demands hard work and constant attention. It's not for the weak or the squeamish or those who'd rather spend their time strolling about in cities than in virgin forest."

"Are you saying I don't fit in, that I might as well go on home?" Tim asked.

"I'm saying . . ." Shakespeare began, and froze when his gaze drifted to the ridge above them where scores of lances and rifles glittered dully in the fading sunlight. "Damn my stupidity," he said.

Tim twisted, sucked in air. "Oh, God! We shouldn't have slowed down! They have us now!"

"Maybe they do," Shakespeare said, facing the drop-off, "and maybe they don't." He reined up and rose as high as he could for a better view of the cliff. It was sheer, the aquamarine water below unmarked by the shadows of submerged boulders. "We just might make it."

"Make what?" Tim said. He saw where the older man was looking, and recoiled as if someone had just suggested that he shoot himself. "You're crazier than I thought if you expect me to do what I think you expect me to do."

"It's either that or let the Crows lift your hair."

"I can't, I tell you!"

A tremendous outcry erupted across the ridge as the Crows hefted their weapons and vented war whoops. With Jacob Pierce in the lead, they swarmed down the slope in bloodthirsty glee.

"Oh, Lord!" Tim bawled.

"Follow my lead," Shakespeare said, turning his horse toward the onrushing Crows. He galloped 20 yards, then reined up in a spray of dust. Higher up, rifles popped, and bullets thudded into the nearby earth. Shakespeare wheeled his mount and galloped straight at the rim. The horse, accustomed to obeying without hesitation, was flailing air before it quite awakened to the peril in which he had placed it. Wind whipped Shakespeare's hair as he pushed off from the animal's broad back and fell free. He saw the surface of the lake growing larger and larger until it seemed to be the whole world, and then he hit, feet first, and cleaved into the water like a blade into flesh, sinking so fast he was completely enveloped in a frigid liquid cocoon in the span of mere heartbeats. The effect was like having a cold fist rammed into his gut, and he almost made a fatal blunder, almost opened his mouth to cry out.

The horse had hit at the same time, the explosion of its impact like the blast of a cannon. Shakespeare saw it above him and to one side, kicking and straining to regain the surface. His momentum had slackened enough that he could do the same, so he drove his legs and arms in short, steady strokes to propel himself upward.

Shakespeare marveled that his bones were still intact. The plunge had rendered the pistol useless but he held onto the gun anyway in case he found a use for it later. The murky depths gave way to lighter water with terrible slowness. His lungs began to ache, and it was all he could do not to gulp in water.

Just when Shakespeare thought he might expire, his head broke through and he gratefully inhaled crisp fresh air. The horse was close by, swimming toward shore. From on high wafted the pop of rifles. Shakespeare glanced up, wondering if the greenhorn would have the gumption to make the jump, and a shadow fell across his upturned face.

With a start, Shakespeare bent at the waist and dived, swimming frantically downward at a sharp angle. He hadn't gone nearly far enough when a second explosion rocked the lake. An invisible hand buffeted him seconds before something more tangible slammed into his shoulder and sent him spinning out of control. He lost all sense of direction. When the spinning stopped, he looked around, trying to determine which way was up. He saw a human figure drifting limply toward him and swam to it. Draping an arm around the greenhorn's chest, he rose to the surface a second time.

Tim Curry came to life, sputtering and wheezing. He coughed in racking sobs and spat water. "Damn you!" he railed. "I nearly got killed!"

"Hush!" Shakespeare warned, letting go. "Follow me. And don't dawdle! We're not out of the woods yet." Instead of making for land, which both horses were now doing, he swam to the base of the precipice and hugged the wall.

The greenhorn paddled up beside him. "What the hell are we doing this for? The shore is in the other direction."

"Keep your mouth shut and take a gander at the rim," Shakespeare said softly.

Tim looked, but saw nothing. He was about to wade into McNair for being the biggest fool in all of creation when over a dozen coppery faces appeared, scanning the lake for sign of them. Tim instantly pressed flush with the smooth rock surface and whispered, "Do you think they'll spot us?"

"Maybe not," Shakespeare said. "We're in the shadow of the cliff. If we're lucky, they'll figure we drowned."

Prominent among the faces was one crowned by a dark beaver hat and wreathed by a bushy beard.

"There's Pierce!" Tim whispered, terrified at the thought of falling into the renegade's clutches again.

"What I wouldn't give for a rifle," Shakespeare said.

The Invincible One and the Crows were most persistent. For ten minutes or better they scoured the lake, only giving up when the setting sun brought darkling twilight to the wilderness. When they disappeared, Tim started to swim out from the cliff wall.

"Not yet," Shakespeare cautioned. "We'll wait another five minutes to be on the safe side."

Treading water, Tim looked landward. "I don't see the horses," he commented. "What if they've gone on back to the village?"

"Then we have a heap of walking to do. But I doubt they've gotten far. A fall like that would have rattled them so badly they'll stay close for a spell."

"At least the savages are gone."

"Not far, they haven't."

"What? Why not? Are they still looking for us?"

"No. Some tribes, the Crows included, think it's bad medicine to be traveling at night. They'll make camp close by and head on back come daylight."

The answer brought home to Tim yet again how very little he knew of the wild and the ways of its inhabitants. Back in Maine he'd often roamed the woods and flattered himself that he was a competent woodsman. His trek westward had been illuminating in that it had demonstrated his ignorance far exceeded his knowledge. Where the Rockies were concerned, he was a virtual babe in the woods. He had grown to doubt the wisdom of his decision to become a free trapper, and thought longingly of the simple, safe life that was his for the asking in the States.

From the forest across the lake wafted a feral shriek that echoed eerily off the cliff. Shakespeare paid it no mind, but Tim Curry glanced at the trees in alarm.

"Was that a mountain lion?"

"Bobcat."

"Are the horses in any danger?"

"Not unless they've shrunk to the size of colts since we saw them last."

Quiet minutes went by, broken only by periodic gusts of wind and the lapping of water against rock. When Shakespeare was satisfied the Crows were long gone, he stroked toward shore at a point where thick brush sloped to the lake's edge. By

then a few stars had blossomed in the heavens and
the water was as black as pitch.

Tim tired swiftly. His drenched buckskins
weighted him down as though they were made
of lead and not deer hide. He was vastly thankful
when his feet at long last brushed the gravel-strewn
bottom. Panting heavily, he shuffled into the undergrowth and sank down beside the older man, who
had squatted to wring water from his clothes.

"Once we find the horses, we'll head north, then
swing westward until we reach the village."

Astonishment brought Tim up off the ground in
a crouch. "I was wrong about you. You're not crazy. You must want to die if you're so all-fired eager
to go back into the lion's den." He gestured irri-
tably. "What could possibly be important enough
to justify the risk? Our supplies? We can replace
them. Our rifles and pistols? We'll manage until
we can buy others."

"I don't care a lick about any of that stuff. It's
Nate King I'm thinking of," Shakespeare answered,
and rose to search the immediate area for their
horses.

"But he got away."

"And so have we, but Nate's probably not aware
of it. And Hamlet isn't the kind to rest until he's
freed us. Even as we speak, he might be spying
on the Crow village, waiting his chance to sneak
on in. He'll be endangering his life for no reason."
So we're going to find him before he does."

"Maybe he saw us ride off."

"I can't take it for granted he did. That boy means
too much to me."

"He's a grown man, not a boy. He can take care
of himself," Tim commented. He didn't like the
idea of going anywhere near the Crow village no
matter what the reason might be, and if not for

the fact he'd be next to helpless on his own without provisions, he would have parted ways with McNair on the spot.

Shakespeare faced the Easterner and replied gruffly, "Get one thing straight, Troilus. Nate King means more to me than you and all the other free trappers put together. I tend to regard him as the son I wish to hell I'd had, and I'd gladly throw my life down for him. He'd do the same for me, for both of us if it came down to it. He's the best there is."

"I didn't mean to upset you."

"Forget it," Shakespeare said, working hard to smother his vexation. The greenhorn's whining and contrary attitude were getting to him, a sure sign he needed rest and recuperation. He walked into the woods, moving silently in order not to spook their mounts. Curry trailed along, and from the racket he made he was doing an outstanding job of stepping on every dry twig in their path.

Movement off to the right drew Shakespeare's interest. A large shape materialized, moving to intercept them. The dull plod of heavy hooves assured him it wasn't a bear. He stopped until the horse halted in front of him, its head hanging. "There, there, fella," Shakespeare said gently. He rubbed its neck and bent to examine its front legs. Neither were broken. Nor were the back ones. The rope reins dangled on the off side, and seconds later he had grabbed them and hooked a leg over the animal's back.

The greenhorn stood gazing forlornly up at him, the perfect picture of city-bred incompetence.

"Here," Shakespeare said, offering a hand. He pulled Curry on behind him, then turned and commenced a systematic hunt of the area around the lake for the other horse. After half an hour he had to concede the animal had strayed off or headed for the village.

"Are we going to look all night?" Tim asked. "I don't mind admitting, I'm bushed. I need rest, McNair, or I'll be of no use to anyone."

Shakespeare would rather have gone on to the village. Unfortunately, their horse was as worn out as the greenhorn. Unless they rested the animal until morning, it wouldn't last long bearing both of them. He rode into a stand of spruce. "You're in luck, Troilus. Pile some pine needles into a pillow and get some sleep."

"Thank you, McNair," Tim said, sliding off.

"Don't thank me. Thank the horse." Shakespeare dismounted and tied the animal where it could graze if it so desired. Out of habit he made a circuit of the stand, verifying all was well. Or as well as things got in the wild, where a man never knew from one minute to the next what new threat would appear. Temporarily, they were safe. They could rest, but they couldn't let down their guard, not unless they didn't care if they wound up in the belly of a roving bear or big cat.

Shakespeare rejoined his companion and found the young trapper snoring lightly. He gazed down on the helpless novice and thought of all the others like Curry who had traveled to the mountains in search of adventure and wealth and wound up as worm food. If their bleached bones were to be stretched out end to end, the skeletal line would reach halfway to St. Louis.

Yet no one could talk them out of throwing their lives away. Shakespeare had sometimes wished there was a magical combination of words that would impress on greenhorns the hard truths of wilderness living. Like sheep flocking to the slaughter, they came west thinking they were fit to deal with Nature on their own terms, only to find out, often too late, that Nature was a tyrant with deaf ears and a heart of ice.

Shaking his head, Shakespeare sat with his back to a trunk and rested the pistol in his lap. He felt along his belt for the knife he'd taken from Two Humps, but it was gone, undoubtedly resting on the bottom of the lake. Since it wouldn't do to be defenseless, he rose again and hunted until he found a broken limb that made a suitable club. Propping it against the tree, he sank down, bowed his chin to his chest, and willed himself to relax so he could fall asleep. The tension filling his body drained, but not the anxiety gnawing at his mind. He was too worried about Nate.

Finally, much later, Shakespeare dozed. He awoke five or six times that night, and would look and listen for a while before drifting off again. His fitful state had one advantage he hadn't foreseen. He was up well before dawn, raring to go.

Shakespeare had to shake the greenhorn vigorously before Tim Curry roused to partial wakefulness. "Rise and shine, Troilus. We have a long ride ahead of us."

Tim smacked his lips while trying to keep his eyes open. "How many times do I have to tell you, McNair? I don't like to be called that."

"Some folks would regard it as an honor to be named after one of old William S.'s characters, but I won't quibble. On your feet."

The horse behaved sluggishly the first mile, but loosened up thereafter. Shakespeare held it to an energetic walk to conserve its strength. He stayed well to the north of the route they had taken the day before and avoided skylines. By the middle of the morning they were winding among a series of low hills laden with briars. Suddenly Shakespeare heard hoofbeats ahead, the drumming of dozens of horses, and reined up.

"It sounds like the Crows," Tim whispered.

Shakespeare eased the horse forward until he could see around the next hill. A large group of Indians were halfway across the narrow plain beyond, bearing to the southwest. The painted symbols on their mounts and their bodies as well as their glittering lances and rifles showed the reason they were abroad. It was a Ute war party. And they were heading for the Crow village.

Chapter Nine

The very instant that Nate King saw the large body of Crow warriors coming toward him, he threw himself backward into the underbrush and ducked low. Ears pricked for an outcry, he tensed to flee should they have discovered him. But there was no reaction; as yet they were too far off.

The chestnut, meanwhile, continued to graze, chomping loudly, unaware of the Indians.

Nate debated whether to crawl to the wayward animal and try to lead it under cover without being detected. He decided it would be unwise to risk being caught in the open, so he cupped his hands to his mouth and called out just loud enough for the horse to hear, "Come this way! Over here, damn your bones! Amble over to the trees!"

The animal looked up, saw him, flicked its ears, and resumed eating.

Just then loud yells broke out. The Crows had spotted the horse. Nate saw some of the warriors peel away from the main group and race forward. He quickly melted into the forest, and ran to the sleeping boy. He gave Gray Badger a shake. The young Crow jumped up as if launched from a catapult and looked around in confusion. "Many warriors from your village are coming," Nate signed. "Do you want them to find you?"

"No," Gray Badger replied.

"Then we must hurry. We will ride double," Nate signed. He turned toward the pack animal, and was flabbergasted to discover the critter was gone. He realized it had strayed off while he searched for the chestnut, and he wanted to kick himself for being so careless, for not tying it again before he left.

Taking the boy by the shoulder, Nate trotted deeper into the woods. He knew the Crows would conduct a search of the immediate vicinity, so he cast about for someplace to hide. There were several thickets, but none dense enough to withstand a close scrutiny. He came to a shallow furrow eroded by rainfall, jumped over it, and kept on going.

Suddenly an idea struck Nate. Turning, he went back to the furrow and examined it closely. Not quite a foot deep and three feet wide, it just might do. Working rapidly, he gathered a number of fallen limbs and broke off several others. "I want you to lie down," he signed to Gray Badger, "so I can cover you."

The boy divined the scheme, and grinned. Reclining on his back in the middle of the furrow, he folded his arms across his chest and held still while Nate aligned branches across the top, hiding him.

Next Nate lay down and covered himself from head to toe. From a distance the branches would blend into the background and appear part of the forest floor. He could only hope none of the Crows came close enough to see that something was amiss.

Shouts presaged the arrival of the warriors. Nate imagined them milling around the horse and trying to figure out what it was doing there and where it came from. One of them was bound to remember his escape and put two and two together. Sure enough, moments later the brush crackled to the passage of horses as the Crows fanned out to scour the woods.

Nate tilted his head to glance at the boy. Gray Badger was as still as stone, a credit to his father's teachings. From an early age Indian boys were taught that the keys to being a successful hunter were patience and the ability to stay motionless for long periods at a time. He was confident the youngster would do nothing to give them away.

Nate shifted again, peering at the trees to the left where the riders were bound to first appear. Presently they did, five somber Crows who probed behind every sizeable bush and poked their lances into every thicket. They were going over every square inch.

Nate held his breath as a skinny brave rode within several yards of the furrow. The man circled a tangle of undergrowth, thrusting with a long lance. Then the Crow moved to the south, his gaze sweeping the woodland ahead but not the ground almost under his mount's hooves.

The warriors hollered back and forth. Nate had no idea what they were saying, nor could he ask the boy. The braves shortly vanished in the vegetation. He prayed that would be the last of them, and was disappointed when three more appeared. Two of the trio came straight toward his hiding place.

Nate closed his eyes until they were slits so the whites wouldn't betray his presence. The farthest Crow slanted to one side, but the nearer Crow rode to the edge of the furrow and there reined up. The man carried a rifle which he rested across his thigh as he arched his back to relieve a kink.

Nate watched the warrior's eyes. They were the key. He saw them swivel right, saw them swivel left. The Crow idly glanced skyward, then shifted and looked down, straight down at the pine boughs covering the furrow, straight at Nate's face. The man's eyes narrowed, his brow furrowed. And then they began to widen in dawning comprehension.

Surging upward, Nate burst through the layer of branches and seized the Crow by the arm. A deft twist, a sharp swing, and the brave sailed through the air into a tree trunk. The warrior's rifle went flying. Nate turned to go get it, but strident yells told him he had already been spotted. In a long stride he reached the man's war horse and swung into the Indian saddle. An arrow streaked past his head as he yanked on the reins.

Nate planned to flee and lead the Crows away from the boy. His good intentions were ruined when Gray Badger abruptly rose, shaking branches from him, and extended his arm. Bending outward, Nate grabbed the boy's hand and swung Gray Badger up behind him as a second arrow fanned his hair. He quickly brought the horse to a gallop, racing for their lives.

Crows seemed to be everywhere. Their whoops and yips resembled a pack of ravenous predators on the blood trail. Nate spotted some on the left and cut to the right. More appeared, so he bore to the right again. And still there were others. The earth seemed to disgorge them in droves.

Nate spotted a warrior raising a rifle. He had nowhere to hide, no way to avoid the shot, so he braced for the searing sensation of the slug ripping through his body. Salvation came from an unexpected quarter as someone bellowed in the Crow tongue, causing the warrior to reluctantly lower his gun. Another brave, about to throw a lance, let his arm drop.

It didn't take a genius to figure out why. Nate guessed that they wanted to take him alive, and they certainly had the odds in their favor, but he'd be damned if he was going to make his capture easy. A Crow came at him with a clawed hand reaching for his arm. Nate dodged, then backhanded the Crow across the mouth and sent the man tumbling.

A shout from Gray Badger drew Nate's gaze over his shoulder. Yet another warrior was bearing down on him with an upraised knife. Nate yanked out the tomahawk he had taken from the dead Crow in the canyon and swung as the knife arced at his face, blocking the swing. The jolt rocked his shoulder. He slashed before the Crow could, slicing deep into the man's chest, and the warrior retreated, bleeding profusely.

Riding with skill surpassed by few, wheeling the horse this way and that, Nate avoided additional enemies. He thought he was doing a fine job of eluding them until his mount suddenly broke from the forest onto the very plain where the chestnut had been grazing and he beheld dozens of warriors clustered directly ahead. They promptly spread out, seeking to enclose him in a howling ring.

Nate reined to the left and galloped northward. The fastest Crows were gaining rapidly, closing in from several different angles. He whipped the tomahawk at one and the man slowed. Another came at him from the opposite side. Nate drove the tomahawk at the Crow's head, but the man jerked away.

Suddenly Gray Badger yelped and his arms slid from around Nate's waist. Nate twisted. A warrior had torn the boy loose and was bearing him off. Without hesitation Nate wheeled his horse to go to Gray Badger's aid, but in doing so he made a grave mistake.

A brash young Crow astride a bay, his face painted red with yellow lightning bolts on both temples, deliberately rode into Nate's mount, the bay's shoulder striking Nate's horse with such gut-wrenching force that Nate's animal crashed to the ground.

Nate leaped clear at the last instant. He scrambled to his feet and drew back the tomahawk to hit his attacker, but had the tomahawk wrenched from his grasp by a warrior who came up on him from the rear. Drawing his knife, Nate leaped and caught hold of the man. The warrior tried to batter him senseless with the tomahawk's haft. Nate thrust at the Crow's stomach, but only succeeded in nicking the skin.

The warrior got a hand on Nate's wrist, then sprang, bearing both of them to the earth. Nate rolled and tried to pull loose. He rose to one knee, and almost had the leverage to rise all the way when additional Crows pounced, flying from their speeding war horses like birds of prey swooping in for the kill.

Nate was buried under an avalanche of warriors. The knife was ripped from him so he fought with fists and feet, knees and elbows. It was a repeat of the fight in the valley, and as in that instance he was doomed to lose. He cracked a jaw, split a lip, and sank knuckles into an unprotected groin.

Then fists rained on him without letup and the whole word spun and danced drunkenly.

Dimly, Nate was aware of iron fingers on his arms and of being brutally yanked to his feet. He sagged and would have fallen if not for the Crows holding him up. His vision slowly cleared to reveal a circle of hostile faces surrounding him, while in front of him stood a bearded white man whose expression was innately more cruel than that of any Crow.

"I lose two, I find two," the man mentioned, evidently talking to himself. "I'd call that a fair swap, I reckon." He jabbed a thick finger at Nate. "You're the one who got away from Whirlwind Hawk, aren't you? What's your name, friend?"

Nate licked his bleeding lips. The Crows must be on amiable terms with some whites, he mused, if this stranger was able to move among them with impunity. So perhaps if he could convince the man that he meant the tribe no harm, they would see fit to release him and restore his possessions. "I'm Nate King," he disclosed. "Who are you?"

"Jacob Pierce."

"Are you a free trapper like me?"

Pierce's mouth curved in a lopsided grin. "This hoss is a trapper, sure enough, but I'm not a thing like you or any other Mountainee Man."

The sarcasm was uncalled for, but rather than take umbrage, Nate said, "Do me a favor and assure these Crows I'm no threat to them. My pards and I weren't even deep in Crow country when Whirlwind Hawk jumped us without cause and took us captive. All we want is to get our fixings back and go on our way in peace."

"I'm sure you do."

Nate scanned the Crows. "I hear tell that a chief by the name of Invincible One has been stirring them up against all whites. Is that true?"

"It sure is."

"Are you a friend of his? Do you know him well?"

"I know him real well."

"Is he crazy? Or just plain stupid?"

Pierce frowned.

"Doesn't he realize that it's better for the Crows if they're our friends, not our enemies? Hasn't he heard about Pierre's Hole, or the Missouri Legion?" The former referred to a pitched battle in which over two hundred whites, two hundred Flatheads, and three hundred Nez Perces had set upon a large force of Blackfeet who had been making trouble for the trappers. The latter referred to the army raised in Missouri to punish the Arikaras for attacking whites. "Talk to him on our behalf and persuade him to smoke the pipe of peace."

"I doubt it would do any good."

"What harm could it do?" Nate persisted. "He has everything to gain and nothing to lose from being on friendly terms with us." Out of habit, Nate lowered his voice. "Is the bastard here now?"

"Yes-sir-ree."

"Which one is he?"

Jacob Pierce shifted in his saddle and seemed to be studying the Crows. He raised a finger and began to point at one, then apparently changed his mind and began to point at another.

"I thought you claimed that you know him," Nate said.

"And I do."

"Then which one is he?"

"This one," Pierce responded, and beamed wickedly while touching the fingertip to his own chest. "I'm the bastard who killed your partners, McNair and Curry."

Nate stiffened in horrified outrage. "Shakespeare? Dead?"

Pierce leaned forward, his features reflecting insolent disdain. "Mercy me. Were you close to the old-timer, King? What a pity." He snickered. "If you can breathe water, you're more than welcome to give the son of a bitch a proper burial."

Where the strength came from, Nate couldn't say. But he abruptly exploded, heaving the Crows from him as if they were feathers, and leaped, getting his hands on Pierce's shirt. Whipping around, he slammed the callous killer to the ground and thought he heard an odd clang. He started to wade into the killer with his fists flying, but the Crows were on him in a flash. Once more he fought them tooth and nail. Fueled by his fury, he knocked down four of them before the others were able to grasp his arms and pin them at his side.

Jacob Pierce had risen, a nasty bruise on his forehead. He took a step forward, eyes blazing, and snaked out his pistol. His thumb curled the hammer back as he pointed the flintlock at Nate's face.

Nate stared death in the face. He squared his shoulders to show the Crows he was unafraid, and met Pierce's glare with a defiant stare of his own. For an eternity the muzzle of the pistol loomed inches from his nose.

"No," Pierce snapped, dropping the hammer. "This would be too simple. You deserve more, King. You deserve to feel pain such as you have never felt before." Pierce jammed the pistol under his belt. "I won't deprive myself of the pleasure of listening to you beg for mercy."

"It will never happen," Nate vowed.

"We'll see."

At an order from Pierce, the Crows slung Nate onto his horse and the whole party trotted westward. Escape was rendered impossible by a living wall of warriors. Nate stayed beside a brave who rode double with Gray Badger, and when they had gone a ways he turned to the boy and signed, "I am sorry. I tried to keep you from falling into their hands and could not."

"You fought like ten men, Grizzly Killer," the boy answered, then added the supreme compliment. "You are as good a warrior as my father."

A Crow riding behind them pulled closer, his hands flowing. "Question? Why does he call you Grizzly Killer? That is an Indian name."

"The Shoshones adopted me into their tribe many winters ago," Nate explained, and would have let the matter drop but the man became surprisingly curious.

"You are Shoshone? We did not know. There has been peace between our two peoples for a long time, and we would not like to have a quarrel with them."

"Tell that to Invincible One."

The Crow dropped back and spoke in hushed tones to several others. Soon the word was being spread among them. Jacob Pierce, unaware of what was going on, rode at the head of the war party with his chin high and his posture rigid, as if he was a victorious Roman centurion returning in triumph.

Nate was pleased by the development, for it could only work in his favor. The Crows and Shoshones, who occupied adjoining territory, had a long-standing truce that neither cared to see violated. Both tribes already had enough enemies to contend with, without having another in each other.

And although Nate was a white man, by being adopted he had become, to all intents and purposes as far as all Indians were concerned, a Shoshone. Indians never did anything halfheartedly. They put their hearts and souls into every enterprise, including adoption. When someone was admitted into a tribe, no matter the color of his skin or his race, then he became a bona-fide member of that tribe subject to the same privileges and discipline as everyone else. The tribe would do anything for him, and he was expected to give equally in return.

Would the Crows risk war with the Shoshones by allowing Pierce to kill him? That was the crucial question Nate pondered as they traveled mile after mile. Pierce did not deign to glance at him even once, not until the village appeared.

"Take a good look, King. You'll never leave it alive."

The moment Pierce faced forward again, Nate used sign language to translate for Gray Badger. Naturally, some of the Crows noticed, and soon Pierce's threat was being passed from man to man.

The entire population turned out for their arrival, the women and children studying the new captive with great interest. Nate was escorted to the same small lodge in which his mentor had been held. His wrists were tied and he was pushed inside and left to his own devices.

Since Nate no longer had to put on a stalwart front for the benefit of the Crows, he moved close to the wall and slumped against it. All the emotion he had kept pent up inside since learning of McNair's death now gushed out from his innermost being, threatening to drown him in profound sorrow. *Not Shakespeare!* Moisture rimmed his eyes, and the only thing that prevented him from bawling like a baby was the knowledge the Crows would hear

and think him weak because grown warriors were
expected to control their feelings at all times.

Still, the anguish was like a red-hot poker burning through Nate's core, and he had to bite down
on his lower lip hard enough to draw blood to
keep from sobbing aloud. Sweet memories filtered
through his mind, of wonderful times spent in the
company of the man he had come to regard as
more of a father than his own had been.

True friends were as rare as gold and were to
be as prized as precious gems. The average person
might have a handful in a whole lifetime, usually less. An affinity of souls, Nate's grandmother
had called such friendships. Rare moments in time
when two people were in harmony. The next best
thing to being married.

Nate knew he would never meet another like
Shakespeare. For all the jesting he had done over
McNair's fondness for the playwright, he would
have given anything to have Shakespeare seated
beside him at that very moment, spouting quota-
tions as glibly as if he had been the one who wrote
the plays.

How much time went by, Nate couldn't say.
Mired in misery, he only roused himself when a
pair of Crows entered, hoisted him to his feet, and
pushed him outside.

The Invincible One and a dozen warriors were
waiting. "Enjoyed your little rest?" Pierce asked.

Nate merely glared, his dislike of the man flaring
into fiery hatred. Had his hands been free, had no
one else been there to stop him, he would have
clamped his fingers on Pierce's thick neck and
squeezed until the killer was as lifeless as McNair.

"I was going to have you run a gauntlet, like
I wanted to do with your friends," Pierce mentioned. "But then I got to thinking. I can use you

to teach the Crows a little lesson. They've been acting a mite uppity of late and I need to put them in their place."

"Killing me won't teach them anything about you they don't already know," Nate responded.

"That's where you're wrong," Pierce said. "They believe my medicine is greater than any man's since I've already demonstrated that I can't be killed. Now I need to show them that I'm as hard inside as I am outside."

"You can't be killed?" Nate scoffed. "Cut me loose and I'll prove you wrong."

"Do you really think I'd be jackass enough to give you the chance?" Pierce said.

The cutthroat spoke in the Crow tongue, and several warriors propelled Nate toward the center of the village. Word must have already spread because it appeared that every last Crow had gathered for the spectacle. Nate foresaw his fate on seeing four stakes imbedded in the shape of a large rectangle. Beside one of them stood a brave holding four long pieces of rope.

Nate wasn't about to submit meekly. He dug in his heels and tried to tear free. More warriors came to the assistance of those holding him, and he was lifted and carried the rest of the way. Nate knew they would have to cut his wrists loose in order to spread-eagle him to the stakes, so he was ready when the loops parted. So were the warriors. The second he began to whip his arms around, four of them were on him, pinning him flat with their combined weight. He heaved and bucked, but his struggles proved useless.

Nate fiercely resisted their attempts to tie him, yet once again their numbers prevailed. His arms were pulled to full extension and his wrists secured. The same was done with his legs. He yanked at the stakes, but couldn't budge them at all. The Crows stood, then moved aside.

Jacob Pierce reared over Nate, wearing a sadistic smile. "Not so cocky now, are you, King? In a few minutes you'll be blubbering hysterically."

"Go to hell," Nate declared.

"After you, I'm afraid," Pierce said, drawing his butcher knife. The blade gleamed brightly in the sunshine as he sank to one knee. "I'm fixing to make me a new ammo pouch. And you get to supply the hide."

Chapter Ten

Nate King had heard stories about men skinned alive. The excruciating torment was said to be unbearable, so overwhelming that some victims went insane from the pain before the skinning was done. Some claimed that it burned, like having the body set on fire after being doused with kerosene. Whatever the case, no trapper in his right mind wished such a terrible fate on his worst enemy.

Nate watched the blade dip toward the bottom of his left leg. He felt a hand grasp his pants, heard the buckskin being slit. The breeze touched his flesh as high as his knee. Then a sharp pang lanced his ankle and he could feel blood trickling down his foot.

Suddenly there was a shout and a quartet of warriors advanced. Two of them addressed Pierce, who jumped up and angrily replied. The warriors, in turn, countered with sharp words and gestures.

At a loss to explain the interruption, Nate craned his neck in order to glimpse his ankle. The knife had just pricked the skin, nothing more. He listened to the argument, trying to determine from facial expressions and motions why the warriors had interferred. As near as he could figure, the Crows didn't want him slain. He suspected it had something to do with the seed he had planted about being an adopted Shoshone, and shortly he had his hunch confirmed when Pierce turned to him in vile wrath.

"What the hell did you tell them, King?"

"I don't know what you mean," Nate said innocently.

"You damned liar!" Pierce fumed, and before Nate could guess the renegade's intent, Pierce hauled off and kicked him in the ribs.

Intense agony speared through Nate's chest. He gritted his teeth to keep from crying out and trembled uncontrollably.

"Pretty damned clever!" Pierce snarled. "Claiming that you're Shoshone because you know the Crows and the Snakes are on friendly terms! Now they don't want me to touch a hair on your head!"

"I am Shoshone," Nate found the strength to say.

"Like hell!" Pierce said, and drew back his leg to kick again. Instead, he glanced at the Crows and slowly lowered his foot. "You're lucky I can't afford to get on their bad side right now, or I'd stomp you to death." Bending over, Pierce grabbed Nate by the throat. "But don't think this lets you off the hook, bastard. You've bought yourself a little time, is all. Tonight I'm holding a council with the chiefs, and when I'm done convincing them, they'll skin you themselves."

Nate didn't respond. Crows cut him loose and hauled him to the small lodge, where he was bound hand and foot and rolled through the doorway. He wormed his way over to the side and pushed himself into a sitting posture. For the time being he was safe, but he couldn't count on the Crows prevailing in the long run. Somehow he had to escape.

Over the next several hours Nate worked diligently at doing just that. He rubbed and rubbed until his wrists and ankles were raw and bleeding. The blood helped to loosen the rope, but not quite enough to permit him to slip a hand free. His feet were another matter. The knife wound added more blood, making his ankles twice as slick. By wriggling and shifting his feet, he was able to finally slide one foot loose.

Now Nate could stand if he wanted, but the exertion had left him weak and woozy. He moved close to the entrance and peeked out. The village lay quiet under the late afternoon sun. A few children played with a hoop. Women were busy at various tasks. One was removing tissue and hair from a buffalo hide. Another was engaged in scraping a hide stretched taut on a square frame. Others were getting an early start on supper by boiling water in buffalo-paunch cooking pots. A few warriors were gambling using buffalo-bone dice.

The Crows were so confident Nate couldn't escape, they had failed to post guards. Not that he would get far if he made a break for it while the sun was up. There were too many Crows abroad, not to mention numerous dogs.

Nate devoted himself to his wrists, chafing them worse as he twisted and slid them back and forth and up and down. The blood flowed thick over his palms and fingers, rendering them sticky. Yet try as he might, he still couldn't free them.

At length the sun hovered above the stark mountains to the west. The village quieted even more as most of the Crows went into their lodges to enjoy their evening meal.

Nate knew the council session would soon be held in the biggest lodge of all. He noticed several warriors dressed in their finest buckskins go in, but saw no sign of the so-called Invincible One. Then, as he shifted for a better view of the council lodge, he detected movement in trees bordering the encampment to the north. Focusing, he saw approximately a dozen warriors, and for a moment assumed they were a hunting party on their way back, until he observed they were moving far too stealthily, slinking from tree to tree, and saw their painted faces and the weapons they held ready for use.

It was a war party! Nate realized. Utes, most likely. And they had slipped past the perimeter sentries and were about to attack. Without thought for his own life, he rose and darted outside, bellowing at the top of his lungs the one word the Crows would understand because it was the same in their tongue and in English. "Utes! Utes! Utes!"

The Crows still outdoors glanced at him, most in puzzled bewilderment. A few, more astute, rose to look around, while from many lodges came curious warriors wanting to know what the uproar was about. And in that frozen moment before the Crows awakened to their plight, the Utes launched their attack.

Screeching and howling like banshees, scores of Utes poured out of the forest in a bloodthirsty wave, clubbing and shooting and stabbing every Crow caught in their path. Over 20 were slain in the first few seconds. Crow warriors were swiftly rallying to defend their loved ones, but as yet the Utes had the upper hand.

Nate was 50 yards from the onrushing line. He knew the Utes would slay him without hesitation. In fact, they would be more eager to kill him since they prized whites' scalps more than those taken from other enemies. So he spun and ran to the south, frantically struggling to slip his wrists from the rope. He passed Crow men charging to the fray. Women and children were fleeing in panic in the same direction he fled. He rounded a lodge, and was on the verge of being in the clear when the high-pitched shriek of a young boy made him look back.

A lone Ute, well in advance of the rest, had clubbed a Crow woman, and was trying to do the same to a young boy resisting furiously. The Ute had the boy by the hair, and was trying to hold him still long enough to slit his throat. The boy was Gray Badger, and there were no Crows nearby to help him.

Whirling, Nate barreled to the rescue. He had no idea what good he could do with his hands bound, but that didn't stop him.

Genuinely brave men never take their own welfare into consideration when they commit acts of raw courage. They simply do what has to be done without regard for the consequences.

The Ute was so busy trying to firm his grasp on the boy that he didn't look up until Nate was almost upon him. Lowering his shoulder, Nate rammed into the Ute's chest, knocking the man into the side of a lodge. The Ute slipped, almost fell, then rallied, and thrust at Nate's heart. Nate jumped backward, and was spared a fatal blow, although the tip of the blade nicked his chest. The enraged Ute came after him, slashing wildly, forcing Nate to retreat before the vicious onslaught. Nate ducked, weaved, leaped aside, always backing away, never slowing. He only had eyes for the glittering knife seeking his life. So it was that he failed to see the aged woman behind him until he collided with her. She had been fleeing, heedless of all else, and had not seen him. Together they toppled in a tangle of legs.

Nate tried to rise quickly, but was hampered by being unable to use his hands. The old woman stood first. She looked down at him and smiled, then bent to grip his shoulders to help him to stand. To Nate's horror, the Ute abruptly appeared behind her, seized her by the hair, and drove his knife into the back of her neck. Nate saw the bloody point slice through the front of her throat, and recoiled as a crimson geyser sprayed him.

The Ute wrenched the knife out, then flung the aged Crow aside. Uttering a bestial growl, he raised his arm for another killing stroke.

Flat on his back, with no time to roll out of the way, Nate did the only thing he could. He drove his right foot into the Ute's knee. There was a loud crack and the warrior staggered to the left. Nate coiled his legs under him and pushed erect just as the Ute recovered sufficiently to stab at him. He skipped out of reach. And when the Ute shuffled in pursuit, he bounded to the right, dropped low, and kicked again, this time into the warrior's other knee.

Hissing like a serpent, the Ute fell. He was in great distress, but not willing to give up. Lunging, he cut at Nate's legs, and Nate leaped high into the air to save himself. On coming down, Nate lashed out with his foot, catching the Ute in the elbow. The man howled when the bone shattered.

Nate danced out of reach and crouched. He tried for the hundredth time to slip his wrists free, but the rope wasn't loose enough. The Ute, teeth grinding, tried to stand, and couldn't straighten his legs. Anxious to end their clash, Nate darted in close to try to kick his enemy in the face. The Ute drove him off with a low swing of the knife.

Desperate circumstances called for desperate measures. Nate had to do something before more Utes appeared. He took a running step forward as if to kick at the warrior's body, and when the Ute attempted to bury the knife in his leg, Nate vaulted high into the air, over the Ute's arm, and rammed the sole of his foot into the Ute's nose. The warrior buckled.

Nate kicked twice in rapid succession, each time planting the sole of his foot on the other's jaw. Groaning, the warrior went limp, and the knife fell from his fingers. Nate crouched beside it, and bent way down so he could grasp the hilt. Reversing his grip, he frantically sawed at the rope.

Meanwhile, a general melee had erupted. The Crows had rallied and were slowly driving the invaders off, but at a high cost. For the most part the battle was being waged man-to-man, although here and there small groups clashed fiercely.

Nate made aggravatingly slow progress. His palms were slippery from blood and sweat, preventing him from getting as firm a hold as he would have liked. Bending his hands as sharply as he could, he cut and cut. Suddenly a hand fell on his shoulder.

With a start, Nate glanced around, dreading it was a Ute out to kill him or a Crow intending to recapture him. But it was neither. Gray Badger took the knife and bent to the ropes, and in seconds they parted. He gave the knife back to Nate, then gestured urgently, signing, "We must get away while we can!"

The crack of guns and the riotous clamor of war whoops had reached a crescendo. Mingled in the din were screams, loud whinnies, and vociferous barking. The Utes had been driven northward to the last line of lodges, but had taken a high toll of the defenders.

Nate ran alongside Gray Badger toward the trees. They passed a dead Crow and Nate saw a rifle lying nearby. It was Shakespeare's Hawken, which Nate promptly claimed. Rolling the Crow over, Nate found Shakespeare's powder horn and ammo pouch. He stripped both off despite the heated urging of the boy to flee.

Once rearmed, Nate sped into the woods. They ran for hundreds of yards, glimpsing clusters of frightened women and children. No one challenged them. The women were too afraid of the Utes to bother about an escaping prisoner.

Once Nate was in the clear, he halted and reloaded the Hawken. It felt grand to have a gun in his hands again. He would have liked nothing better than to encounter Jacob Pierce and demonstrate to the Crows their folly in believing any man impossible to kill.

"We must keep going," Gray Badger signed. "Once the Utes have been driven off, Invincible One will send men to hunt us."

"I am not running," Nate signed.

"What will you do?"

"Find Invincible One and kill him."

Gray Badger clutched at his throat in dismay. "He can not be slain! Many have tried, many have died. We are better off running."

"There comes a time when a man must stand and fight if he is to be worthy of being called a man," Nate said. "My belongings, my horses, and my guns were taken from me because of Invincible One. The only way I will get them back is if I show your people that my medicine is more powerful than his."

"You will be killed," Gray Badger signed sadly, "and then I will be all alone again."

"We will find your father."

"Why?" the boy responded. "If he cared for me, he would have searched for me before now."

"Maybe Invincible One would not let him," Nate speculated. "Until we learn the truth, you must trust in your father to do what is right." He gave the young Crow a pat of encouragement on the head, but Gray Badger was beyond being cheered by words or gestures.

"I want you to stay here until I return," Nate signed. "If I am not back by dark, you will be on your own."

"I do not want you to leave me."

"I have no choice," Nate signed, and ran northward. He assumed Pierce would be helping the Crows drive off the Utes, and since it sounded as if heavy fighting still raged on the north side of the village, he figured that was where he would find the renegade. He passed a few bunches of women and children who either fled or cowered in brush until he had gone by.

As the tumult increased, Nate slowed and angled toward the lodges. He came to a log and hunkered behind it to survey the landscape ahead. Five or six of the teepees were in flames. Dozens of Crows and Utes lay scattered about, some moving, some not, some groaning or wailing, others bearing their wounds in stoic silence.

Beyond the northernmost dwellings a running fight was underway. The Utes were retreating in an orderly manner, pockets of them keeping the Crows at bay while the majority gained ground on their vengeful pursuers.

The raid had been different than most, Nate reflected as he advanced again. Usually a warring tribe conducted a lightning foray, fleeing before many lives were lost. Some tribes considered it the very worst of calamities for a single brave to die on a raid. But this time the Utes had been out for blood, and hadn't seemed to care about losing many of their own. Nate didn't know what to make of their strategy.

About 60 yards away a half-dozen Utes were putting up stiff resistance against twice that many Crows. Arrows and lead flew back and forth.

Nate stopped at a fir tree, braced the Hawken against the trunk, and took precise aim on a Ute with a bow. His shot felled the man as the Ute started to release a shaft. Nate was reloading when the Crows made a concerted rush and put the Utes to flight.

Treading warily forward along the tree line, Nate sought sign of Jacob Pierce. He was beginning to think Pierce had elected to remain out of the fray when a familiar raspy voice bellowing orders in the Crow tongue drew him toward a jumbled maze of downed timber. Somewhere in there, he knew, was the rogue.

Alert for Utes, Crows, and Pierce, Nate cautiously clambered over downed trees and crept through dense growth. The acrid scent of gunsmoke hung heavy in the air. He found a dead, scalped Ute, then another with eyes gouged out. From the trampled vegetation and puddles of fresh blood, it was clear a ferocious clash had taken place.

Presently, through the trees, Nate saw several Crows stalking to the northeast. Pierce wasn't among them. Nate moved to the left, around a large stump, and halted, his blood chilling, as 30 feet off the killer appeared. Pierce shouted more instructions, then worked at reloading a rifle.

Nate didn't dare miss the golden opportunity fate had presented. He tucked the Hawken to his shoulder, sighted down the barrel, and pulled back the hammer with his thumb. Very carefully, he fixed the front bead on Pierce's back, and hesitated. Shooting a man from behind was a cowardly act, plain and simple. He wanted Pierce to turn, wanted Pierce to know what was coming.

The Invincible One finished loading and straightened. He shouted, started to walk deeper into the woods. In another few steps he would be lost in the vegetation.

Nate sucked in his breath, steadied the Hawken, and yelled, "Over here, you son of a bitch!" Pierce, predictably, whirled, and the instant the bead settled on the center of the killer's chest, Nate squeezed the trigger. He grinned as Jacob Pierce was lifted from his feet and flung into high grass.

"So much for being invincible!" Nate said under his breath. Dashing behind the stump, he reloaded, then glided toward the spot where Pierce had fallen. He couldn't wait to show the Crows that no one deserved so lofty a name, and to persuade them to return all of the goods stolen from his trapping party. He would take all of McNair's possessions to his friend's Flathead wife. Curry's things he would sell and send to the greenhorn's next of kin.

Nate came to where Pierce had been standing and looked down, expecting to find drops of blood. There were none. He went further, into the grass, to where the body should have been, but there was no body, just an impression in the grass where something heavy had fallen.

"What in the world?" Nate blurted out, and raised his head to scour the area. The glint of sunlight off metal saved his life, for it gave him the fraction of a second warning he needed to dive to the right. A rifle boomed and the slug whizzed overhead.

Nate rolled in among small pines and rose partway. He was amazed Pierce had survived. At that range Nate rarely missed. But obviously he had, or else the ball had merely grazed the killer and not drawn much blood. Either way, he intended to put a stop to Pierce's bloody career then and there.

Bearing to the right, Nate sank onto his elbows and knees and crawled. Pierce would need up to a minute to reload, giving Nate time to sneak in close enough for a fatal shot. He snaked through the pines to more grass, through the grass to a tall bush. Tucking both knees up under him, he rose high enough to catch sight of someone moving through waist-high weeds 20 feet away. He took a hasty bead, but never saw the figure clearly enough to tell who it was, and held his fire.

Lowering to the ground, Nate crawled to the northeast, to a pine. He stood in the shelter of the wide trunk and peered out. The wily Pierce was nowhere to be seen. Nate wondered if the renegade was hiding somewhere, waiting for whoever had taken the shot to show. Glancing down, he saw a short piece of broken limb and picked it up. The trick he was about to try was as old as the hills, but sometimes still worked.

Nate hurled the stick as far as he could to the south, then brought the Hawken to his shoulder while scanning the vegetation on all sides. The stick hit with a thud, rustling some weeds. Almost immediately a dark shape materialized beside a spruce to the west and the man shot at the weeds. The shooter's face was in shadow, but a stray ray of waning sunlight bathed his head, revealing a beaver cap. Nate aimed and fired. The Hawken belched a cloud of gunsmoke that momentarily hid Pierce. By the time the smoke cleared, Pierce was gone.

Pressing his back to the pine, Nate reloaded rapidly. He had no idea whether his shot had been accurate, and there was only one way to find out. Crouching, he raced in a half circle that brought him up on the spruce from the rear. He probed the grass at its base and nearly cursed aloud. Again there was no body!

Mystified, Nate cat-walked to the left, to a small boulder. Squatting, he examined the Hawken's sights, but they were fine. He couldn't understand how he could have missed a second time. A troubling notion, unbidden, filled his head: What if Jacob Pierce really was invincible? He shrugged, dismissing the idea as lunacy. Yet how else could he account for the rogue's deliverance? He had never thought to inquire why the Crows believed Pierce to be immortal, and they must have had a good reason.

Nate might have stayed there pondering for minutes had a twig not snapped. Twisting, he gazed in the direction the sound came from, but saw no one. He propped the rifle on the top of the boulder, and pulled the hammer to be ready in case it was Pierce or an Ute. Then he thought he saw something move, but he couldn't be sure.

Brush suddenly parted, revealing a buckskin-clad forearm. For a minute nothing else happened. At last the forearm moved, parting the brush wider, and Jacob Pierce showed himself from the waist up. He was staring north of Nate's hiding place, at a thicket he evidently believed harbored Nate.

This time Nate had the butcher right where Nate wanted him. He willed himself to calm down, to still his speeding pulse. He took twice as long as he normally would to set the bead on the exact middle of Pierce's torso. His finger delicately touched the cool metal trigger, and he held the Hawken rock steady for all of five seconds before he fired.

Pierce clutched at his chest and fell backward into the brush. Nate sprinted madly toward the spot, afraid he would get there and find Pierce had once more evaporated into thin air. He was yards off when he saw the foot, and smiled. Plunging into the brush, he stood over Pierce and beamed in elation at his victory. Only belatedly did he see there was no blood. Only belatedly did he see that Pierce still held a rifle. He leaned down to pry the gun from the dead man's fingers, and as his fingers closed on the barrel Pierce's eyes snapped wide open and the killer's other hand closed on his ankle.

Chapter Eleven

Total paralyzing shock held Nate King in place, and Jacob Pierce was quick to take advantage. The killer gave a vicious wrench, causing Nate's leg to sweep out from under him. As Nate crashed down, Pierce shifted, trying to bring his rifle to bear. In sheer reflex Nate swung the Hawken, and swatted the renegade's rifle aside just as the gun discharged.

They both rose to their knees. Pierce growled and attempted to smash Nate in the head, but again Nate parried. Angered by his failure, Pierce began raining blows down in a furious attempt to smash Nate's skull to a pulp. The two barrels tinged together repeatedly. Then, swiveling, Nate lanced the muzzle of the Hawken into the killer's gut, doubling Pierce over in sputtering agony.

Seizing the initiative, Nate gained his knees and drew back the Hawken to club his foe. But Pierce was far from defenseless, and he abruptly let go of his rifle and leaped, clamping his arms fast on Nate's chest and bearing Nate to the ground. Pierce grabbed the Hawken, and they struggled mightily for possession. Nate was about to wrest it loose when the killer kneed him in the groin.

Racked by a welling wave of anguish, Nate sagged, weakening. He clung to the Hawken for dear life as Pierce tugged and jerked. The renegade bent toward him to get a better purchase on the rifle, and the moment Pierce did, Nate rammed his forehead into the other's face. Pierce slumped, blood oozing from his nose, and Nate rammed him again.

Jacob Pierce lost his grip on the rifle and fell to one side. Nate would have sorely liked to bash in the man's brains, but his groin still throbbed abominably, the misery rendering him too feeble to lift the Hawken. He fell back onto his haunches, and resisted an instinctive impulse to bend over and cup his privates. He had to keep fighting! He mustn't give in to the pain or he would die!

Pierce was slowly pushing off the ground. Nate forced his legs to cooperate, and beat the rogue to the punch. Swaying, he held the rifle as if it were a club and streaked it overhead. Pierce glanced up just as Nate swung, and hurled himself aside. The stock clipped the killer on the temple, stunning him.

Nate took a shambling stride and lifted the Hawken again. Pierce looked up in horror, aware of Nate's intention but incapable of doing a thing.

"Here's where I end it," Nate said. He looked into Pierce's eyes and saw a sight that gave him deep, personal satisfaction: fear, raw, unbridled fear. He began his swing.

Unexpectedly, the underbrush crackled and three Crows were there. They leaped on Nate, knocking him off his feet, trapping him under them as they smashed him flat. He hit one with the stock, and was punched in the cheek by another. In concert they held his arms down and the Hawken was ripped from his grasp. Nate kneed the warrior astride his chest, then tried to kick the man on his right.

From out of the woods dashed a fourth Crow, holding a fusee. Cocking the trade gun, he touched the barrel to Nate's nose and barked words in his tongue.

Nate didn't need a translator. He stopped resisting and was yanked erect. He saw a tall Crow offer Pierce a hand, but Pierce angrily slapped it away and stood on his own.

"I'm making you a promise here and now, King. Before the sun comes up tomorrow, you're gone beaver."

Nate stared at the renegade's shirt, looking for blood or bullet holes. All he found were two tiny rips level with the sternum.

"Did you hear me?" Pierce snapped when he received no answer. "Don't you have anything to say?"

"How?" Nate asked.

"How what?"

"I put three balls into you. Had you dead to rights each and every time. Yet there aren't any wounds. How can that be?"

Some of Pierce's former bluster returned. "Wouldn't you like to know, you rotten varmint! But it'll be a cold day in hell before I tell you. The secret of my medicine goes to my grave with me."

At a command from the Invincible One, the Crows shoved Nate toward the village. By now the battle was over, the attackers having been routed, but not before wreaking a terrible toll on the defenders. Crows were going from body to body, helping hurt friends and taking the few Utes found alive back to the village.

Halfway to the village the four warriors escorting Nate were approached by several others and a heated debate broke out. Nate had no idea why they were arguing, but soon suspected he was the cause when several pointed at him while making statements. Then Pierce appeared and sent the newcomers packing. As they left, the Invincible One spun and jabbed Nate with a finger.

"You think you're so damn clever, don't you?"

"I have my moments," Nate quipped, when in truth he didn't have the vaguest notion what Pierce was talking about.

"Well, it's not going to work. I won't let you turn these stupid savages against me, not when I'm just a few trapping seasons away from being one of the richest men in the country. Your killing a few Utes won't change a thing."

Nate was ushered onward, giving him time to reflect on the comment. Apparently some of the Crows had seen him trying to save Gray Badger from the Ute in the village, or else had witnessed him shooting the Ute with the bow. If word spread, it would reinforce the case of those Crows who wanted him spared.

Nate reached the edge of the trees, and observed women and children returning in droves. Mournful cries filled the air as loved ones were found lying in pools of blood. One elderly woman knelt beside her slain son, beating her temples with her fists. The next moment she had taken her son's knife, poised it over her hand, and sliced off one of her fingers as a token of the depth of her grief.

At the small lodge Nate received a surprise. Instead of being tied, he was simply pushed inside, and one of the Crows addressed him in sign language.

"We will leave you on your honor, Grizzly Killer, if you will promise not to escape."

"Why would you do this for me?" Nate asked.

"We have heard how you fought to save the young boy. We know now that you are not the enemy Invincible One would have us believe you are."

"Then I give you my word," Nate signed, "but on one condition."

"Speak."

"Tell everyone you meet that I am a friend and hold no ill will against the Crows for the way I have been treated. It is Invincible One who is to blame, for he has filled your heads with lies and deceived you into thinking he cannot be killed."

"We have seen with our own eyes that weapons have no more effect on him than drops of rain."

"He tricks all of you."

"How?"

"That I do not know, but I will before too long."

The Crow grunted. "I am Big Hail. Two Humps is my friend. I will do as you want, and so will some of the others. At the council later I will speak in your behalf."

"If Big Hail does this for me, then is he my friend as well," Nate signed, and received a warm smile. He watched the warriors trot off, and took a seat just inside the entrance, his shoulder leaning on the lodge. The events of the past hour or so had left him greatly fatigued, and he dearly wanted to lie down and sleep. Yet he couldn't, not when he didn't know if he would wake up again; he wouldn't put it past Pierce to slit his throat while he slept.

The general lamentation had grown loud enough to be heard a mile off. As was typical among most tribes, the women were the ones who expressed their grief vocally. The men reflected their sorrow in sad countenances, but did not cry out.

Both sexes indulged in other practices as well. One was the chopping off of fingers from the first joint up, as the elderly woman had done. Another custom was for mourners to take arrows and lightly stab themselves in a straight line across their foreheads from ear to ear. The men also pricked their arms, legs, and torsos, and some did it so many times their bodies were covered with thin scarlet rivulets. The females made a point of smearing their faces with blood, a tradition that demanded they must not wash until the blood had completely faded.

A few chose less painful methods. Shaving the hair close to the head was done, but infrequently. The war horses of chiefs and prominent warriors were also shaved, and the manes and tails wrapped in bundles and buried with the deceased, it being a Crow belief that the hairs would turn into horses in the spirit realm.

Presently all the wounded Utes, seven in number, were brought into the village. And then Nate was treated to an uncommon spectacle as the Crows took revenge on their enemies. Easterners would have branded the treatment the Utes received as barbaric in the extreme, but the Crows did no worse than would have been done to them had the situation been reversed.

The Utes were laid out in a row and completely surrounded. The Crows held the first captive down while one of their number wielded a razor-sharp knife with marvelous dexterity. The Ute's ears were sliced off and dangled in front of his eyes. Then his nose was chopped off, and each finger and toe, one at a time. He was scalped prior to having his stomach slit and his intestines pulled out. Last, the Crow gouged the Ute's eyes from their sockets and threw them to the onlookers, who played catch with them until the novelty wore off.

The whole time the carving took place, the Crows kept up a scornful verbal abuse of their prisoners. There was much yelling and whooping, and those so inclined picked up discarded body parts and tossed them in the Ute's face.

Most amazing of all to Nate was the captive's ability to endure the torture without complaint or sign of weakness. Not once did a sound pass the Ute's lips, not even when the lips themselves were hacked off. Until the very end the Ute showed his courage and manhood. He finally expired when his heart was cut from his chest.

The other Utes had observed everything. Yet not one flinched when his time came. Not one called out, or cried, or did anything that would besmirch the reputation of his tribe.

At the end, all the heads were chopped off and jammed onto poles which the women took and waved about. When they'd had enough, they smashed the heads on rocks and scattered the brains outside the camp for beasts to eat. The same was done with the bodies of the Utes, except for one. It was tied to a tree, and the children were allowed to amuse themselves by shooting arrows and throwing small lances into it. By the time the children tired of their sport, the body resembled a porcupine.

Night had descended when the Crows dispersed to attend to their own dead. Nate's eyelids were growing heavy, and he put a hand to his mouth to stifle a yawn. Suddenly a small figure appeared and boldly stepped up to him.

"Good evening, Grizzly Killer. I saw them bring you in and have come to stand by your side."

Nate blinked in surprise, grabbed Gray Badger's shoulders, and pulled the boy in. "What are you doing here?" he signed. "You should have been far away by now."

"I started to go," the boy responded. "But your words hung in my head and I could not shake them out." He paused, then repeated the statement Nate had made earlier. "There comes a time when a man must stand and fight if he is to be worthy of being called a man."

"But I did not mean you should put yourself in danger on my account."

"What kind of friend would I be if I left you to face Invincible One alone?"

Nate didn't know whether to be flattered or angered. He glanced out, but saw no indication that anyone had noticed Gray Badger arrive. "I want you to leave. Go find your father. I am sure he will stand up for you."

"I will stay with you, my friend," the young Crow signed.

"Like hell," Nate said aloud, and gripping Gray Badger's wrist, he hauled the boy through the opening and gave him a push. "Go before you are seen. You can do more good for me if you tell your father that I am your friend and ask his aid."

"My father no longer cares about me."

"You are wrong. I am a father. So I know that in their hearts all fathers care for their sons, even if they do not always show it as often as they should." Nate put a hand on Gray Badger's shoulder. "There is something else you must keep in mind. A man can be measured by the quality of his children. You are a boy I would be proud to call my own, which means your father must be a wise man to have raised you so well. And no man could raise so well who loves so little. I think you do him an injustice, and I think it is time you found that out for yourself. Go home."

Gray Badger hesitated.

"Go home," Nate repeated. He folded his arms, and watched the boy run toward a lodge at the far end of the circle. A half-dozen fires had been lit, providing more than enough illumination for him to see that Gray Badger made it safely. The Crows were preparing for a special ceremony to commemorate the passing of their fellows, and would be up until dawn dancing and singing and chanting. Over in the council lodge a meeting was underway, the purpose of which wasn't hard to guess.

No one was paying Nate any regard. He could have left if he wanted, could have turned and faded into the forest without any of the Crows being the wiser. But he had given his word, and he solemnly believed that once a man had done so, nothing short of death must make him break it. He moved back into the small teepee and sat with his back to the wall.

The drone of voices and crackling of flames had a soothing effect. Nate dozed despite himself, and would not have awakened until morning, or perhaps never if Pierce had gotten to him first, had a small hand not gingerly touched his wrist. He snapped upright and shifted.

Gray Badger knelt next to him. The boy's features were in shadow, but there was no mistaking the glistening streaks on his cheeks.

"I thought you went home," Nate signed. "Why are you back so soon?"

"My father is gone."

"Where?"

"He is searching for me," Gray Badger replied, his hands shaking a little as he formed the symbols. He made a choking sound and went on. "My mother told me he has been out of his mind with worry. He wanted to come after me, but he is one of the few men brave enough to stand up to Invincible One, and he was worried about what Invincible One might do in his absence. So he sent his friend, Whirlwind Hawk, to find me."

"I told you."

"There is more," Gray Badger signed, and had to stop to clear his throat. "Invincible One has accused my father of having a hand in helping your friends escape."

Nate was all interest. "Why?"

"My mother says that Wolverine used my father as a hostage to keep the other men from shooting. Later, the warriors found tracks that showed my father had parted company with your friends without being harmed. Some tried to follow his trail, but lost it."

"You met Wolverine. He is not the kind to kill a hostage for no reason. He just let your father go his way in peace."

"Invincible One will never believe that."

Another possibility occurred to Nate. Since Two Humps had been a thorn in Pierce's side for some time, Pierce might have been looking for any excuse to turn the Crows against him. But the incident Pierce had picked smacked of desperation, for the Crows were not about to turn on one of their own chiefs without convincing proof of wrongdoing on the chief's part.

"I am afraid for my father," Gray Badger signed.

"You have nothing to fear. Two Humps would not be a chief if he was not a skilled warrior. He can stand up to Invincible One."

"But what if Invincible One challenges my father in public? My father would be killed as so many others have been."

The thought that struck Nate brought a somber smile to his lips. "I have an idea," he signed, and then went on to detail a request.

"Your mind must be in a whirl for you to think of such a thing," Gray Badger remarked. "No one can kill him. I know. I have seen his medicine work with my own eyes."

"My medicine is stronger," Nate boasted. "And I can prove it if you will do as I say."

The boy looked out at the council lodge. "It is forbidden for anyone to interrupt when the council is meeting," he signed nervously.

"Would you rather have your father come back and be accused by Invincible One of being a traitor to his own people?"

Gray Badger gnawed on his lower lip. "Are you doing this to save my father? He would not want any man to fight his fights for him."

"I am doing this for me," Nate said as he stood, "and for every other trapper in these mountains. Invincible One must be stopped before more whites lose their lives and their furs." He paused. "But most of all I am doing this for Wolverine. He was the best friend I have ever had, and I can not let his death go unpunished."

"You cared for him very much."

"We all make a lot of friends during a lifetime. But a few, a very few, are so special they are too deep for words to describe. Wolverine and I were like that."

"Then you should have your chance to avenge him," Gray Badger said, and hastened away.

Nate stepped outside, into the inky shadows to the right of the flap, and sat cross-legged with his back to the lodge. He imagined he would not have long to wait, and he was right. Within minutes a heated quarrel had broken out in the council lodge. Many Crows stopped whatever they were doing to listen.

In due course warriors began filing out. Jacob Pierce was the last to emerge. He had a firm hand on Gray Badger's arm, and roughly shoved the boy ahead of him every step of the way as the entire party came to the small lodge. Pierce pushed Gray Badger so violently that the boy stumbled, then knelt to look inside.

"I'm over here," Nate said softly.

Pierce spun and stabbed a hand at one of his pistols. He stopped when he saw that Nate posed no threat, and slowly straightened. "What the hell are you up to now, King? You ought to be ashamed of yourself. Sending the brat to do a man's work!"

"What's your answer?" Nate asked.

Pierce folded his arms and glowered. "I'm in no mood to humor you. My answer is no. Why should I soil my hands when you're not worth the bother? You proved that earlier."

"Showing your true color at last," Nate taunted, and regarded the gathered members of the council. "What did the Crows have to say about my challenge?"

"Most of them side with me."

"Do they?" Nate said, and before the renegade could intervene, he resorted to sign language to address the Crows. "Honorable warriors, I greet you in friendship," he began formally. "I came to this country wanting only to trap beaver, yet because of Invincible One I have been forced to strike at those my people regard as brothers. Is this right, I ask you? Should you let Invincible One carry on as he has, killing whites without cause and antagonizing those who are your friends?"

"Why you . . . !" Pierce snarled, advancing. He almost had his pistol out when one of the Crows said something that caused him to abruptly halt.

"In your hearts you know that he has led you astray," Nate continued. "You know that your people would be better off without him. If you will let me, I will rid you of him once and for all. I will show you that his medicine is an illusion."

Jacob Pierce could bear no more. Leaping, he caught hold of Nate's shirt with one hand and whipped out his flintlock with the other. He jabbed the barrel at Nate and pulled back the hammer, but before he could fire Nate batted the gun aside, swept up off the ground, and gave Pierce a powerful push that propelled the renegade back into the Crows. The pistol discharged into the ground. A few of the warriors tried to grab Pierce's arms, but the furious rogue shook them off and stormed forward.

"All right, King! You get your wish! But since you issued the challenge, I get to pick the weapons. And I choose tomahawks!" Pierce tramped off, shouting over his shoulder. "In one hour in the middle of the village. I'll be waiting."

The confused Crows stared after him, then at Nate, who signed, "Invincible One has accepted. In a short while we will fight with tomahawks." He went inside as murmuring broke out behind him. Soon the news would spread from one end of the village to the other. The entire population was likely to turn out to see the fight, which didn't bother Nate in the least. What *did* bother him was Pierce's choice of weapons. Why tomahawks, he wondered, when Pierce had already demonstrated that bullets had no effect on him?

A small form filled the doorway. "I hope you know what you are doing, Grizzly Killer," Gray Badger signed. "I would not like to lose the first white friend I have ever had."

Nate grinned. "Thank you. As to whether I know what I am doing, ask me when it is over."

"You sound worried."

"I am." Nate beckoned the young Crow to take a seat. "You mentioned seeing Invincible One fight before. Have you ever seen him use a tomahawk?"

"No. But he went on a raid against the Blackfeet once to show us that they could not kill him. My father went along. During the raid he saw a Blackfoot swing a tomahawk at Invincible One's chest."

"What happened?"

"Invincible One was knocked down but got right up again. He hit the Blackfoot on the mouth with his fist and the Blackfoot fell. Then he took the tomahawk. As the Blackfoot went to stand, Invincible One buried the tomahawk in his head."

"Was Invincible One bleeding afterward?"

"No. But he did walk slowly for a while."

Nate began pacing, a habit of his when under great stress. Evidently the renegade was as impervious to tomahawks and knives as he was to rifles and pistols. But there had to be a way to kill the bastard, and he would find it or die trying.

"Is there anything I can do to help you?" Gray Badger signed.

"Only one that I can think of," Nate responded, and crouched in front of the boy. "You can do me a great favor if I am slain."

"How?"

"Find a way of getting word to the Shoshones, to the village of Chief Broken Paw. I would like my wife and children to know my fate."

"You can depend on me," Gray Badger signed.

"I thank you. Now leave me. I have much to think about."

The boy complied, but it was clear he was loath to do so. Nate lowered the flap and sat in the darkness reminiscing, thinking of his loved ones, of his life in general. It was rare for him to have such a luxury before a conflict. The dangers of wilderness living were so plentiful and so varied that usually he was embroiled in a fight for his life without any advance warning whatsoever. He'd often dreaded that one day he might be shot from ambush, or ripped in half by a ravenous grizzly before he had time to so much as blink, and he'd wind up dying without having time to think about Winona or Zach or Evelyn.

The hour elapsed swiftly. Immersed in fond recollections, Nate had no idea it had gone by until he heard his name being bellowed. Stepping to the flap, he shoved it wide open, and wasn't at all taken aback to behold scores upon scores of Crows formed into a wide circle with an opening on the side facing the small lodge. Through the gap he could see his nemesis, waiting with a tomahawk in each hand.

Nate strode briskly to meet Pierce. The renegade had changed into a baggy buckskin shirt several sizes too big. Why, Nate had no idea. He walked up to the Invincible One and held out his right hand. "I'm ready if you are."

"You think you are, but I'll soon show you otherwise," Pierce said, extending his left arm. "This one is for you."

Gripping the haft, Nate hefted the tomahawk a few times, gauging its weight and balance. It was a superior weapon, made by a Crow expert at the craft.

"I can't tell you how much I've looked forward to this. Once I dispose of you, things can go back to the way they were," Pierce declared bitterly.

"Big talk when you haven't even gotten in the first lick yet."

"Then it's time I did," Pierce said, and executed a lightning strike that would have split Nate's face had Nate not skipped backward with a hair to spare.

Thus the fight was joined. Nate countered by swinging at Pierce's legs, but the renegade jumped from the blade's path. Pierce aimed a terrific blow at Nate's head, which Nate blocked. Then, in a downward motion, Nate tried to rip open Pierce's abdomen. Again Pierce evaded the swing.

The two combatants separated and circled, taking the measure of one another. Nate was slightly bigger, but he didn't delude himself into thinking that gave him any sort of edge. He feinted, forcing Pierce backward, and it was then, when Pierce raised his tomahawk to ward off the presumed attack, that Nate noticed he had been duped. *The handle of Jacob Pierce's tomahawk was four or five inches longer than his!*

The discovery jolted Nate so severely that he almost had his head separated from his shoulders. Only his pantherish instincts saved him. He backed off an extra stride, mad at himself for not realizing it sooner. Four or five inches wasn't much, but it was enough to give Pierce a longer reach, a wider swing. It was enough to cost Nate dearly in flesh and blood.

Pierce wore that aggravating smirk of his as he waded in close once more. He drove his tomahawk at Nate's chest, and when Nate spun out of reach,

Pierce reversed direction and went for Nate's neck. Their tomahawks clashed, parted, clashed once more.

Nate ducked to the right, staying well beyond the radius of his foe's reach. His tactic appeared to upset Pierce, who was transparently eager to end their fight quickly. Pierce's tomahawk cleaved the air, narrowly missing the top of Nate's head. For a second Pierce left his chest exposed, and Nate instantly struck. The edge of his tomahawk tore into the baggy buckskin shirt but *glanced off Pierce's body!*

The renegade staggered rearward, regained his balance, and sneered. "You'll have to do better than that, bastard!"

Nate was at a loss to know what to do. With his shorter reach he would be hard pressed to wound Pierce in the arms or legs. And with Pierce's chest virtually invulnerable, it seemed as if the outcome was foreordained. Then he remembered the one time he had hurt Pierce, when they had first met and he'd bruised Pierce's forehead. In a flash of inspiration the simple answer to his dilemma exploded full-blown in his brain and made him grin.

"What can you possibly find so funny?" Pierce demanded.

"Just this," Nate said. He had been circling to the right. Suddenly he circled to the left instead, throwing Pierce off stride. Dropping into a crouch, he swung at the renegade's knees. Pierce automatically hopped backward, and as he did, Nate flung himself forward, his left forearm rising to block Pierce's counter-swing even as he slashed his tomahawk in an overhand blow that ended with the blade cleaving into Pierce's skull. It sheared through hair, through skin, and deep into the underlying bone, so deep Nate couldn't pull it out again, so he let go and backed away.

Jacob Pierce's eyelids fluttered as he tottered to the left, his arms swinging feebly, a dull groan coming from his parted mouth. Blood poured down over his face, covering his eyes, his nose, his lips. He sputtered, began to reach upward, then froze for a few seconds before keeling over with a loud thud.

The Crows gaped in astonishment, and it was obvious from their expressions that many fully expected the renegade to rise and continue the fight.

Nate inhaled slowly, calming himself. He stepped to the body, pulled Pierce's knife from its sheath, and slit Pierce's buckskin shirt up the middle. In the pale glow of the flickering firelight a large, thin sheet of steel was exposed, attached by leather straps to Jacob Pierce's chest and shoulders. The sheet bore dozens of nicks, scrapes, and dents where it had been hit by knives, arrows, and bullets. "Well, I'll be damned," Nate said to himself. Rolling the body over, he pulled up the shirt high enough to reveal a similar sheet that covered Pierce's back from the shoulder blades to the waist.

A small Crow detached himself from the throng and walked over. Nate glanced at Gray Badger, tapped the steel, and signed, "So much for the Invincible One."

"He will never rise again?"

"Not in this life."

"No one will miss him. His medicine was as bad as his heart. What good can be said about a man like him?"

"In the end, he got what he deserved."

Epilogue

It was one week later that Nate King, Shakespeare McNair, and Tim Curry rode from the Crow village with all their horses and their possessions intact. McNair and Curry had shown up the day after the death of the Invincible One, after Shakespeare had spotted Nate strolling about the village as if he owned the place. And in a sense, Nate did.

The Crows could not apologize often enough to suit them. They did their best to accord him all hospitality, and assured him again and again that they were staunch friends of the trappers and the Shoshones.

To make matters perfect, on the second evening after the fight, Two Humps rode in from the south, dejected because he had failed to find his son. The reunion brought tears to many an eye. And with Pierce's deceit proven, Two Humps's public esteem rose higher than ever.

Now, with the sun shining down on the verdant countryside, Nate reined up on a hill for a last look at the village. "I suppose it was all worthwhile in the end," he commented.

"If nothing else, we've shown those Crows that not all whites are no-account, murdering sons of bitches," Shakespeare said.

"This nightmare has taught me something as well," Tim Curry said. "I hope you won't be upset, but I plan to head on back to the States and take up where I left off in Maine. There's a nice, safe job waiting for me there, and I can take a walk in the woods whenever I want without having to worry about being parted from my hair."

Shakespeare chuckled. "Do you mean to tell us you'd give up all the excitement of wilderness living for a plain, safe, civilized life?"

"Do you hold it against me?"

"Not at all, young Troilus." Shakespeare patted his parfleche. "If there's one thing old William S. has taught me, it's this." He paused to sort through his memory. "This above all, to thine own self be true."

WILDERNESS

Fang & Claw
David Thompson

To survive in the untamed wilderness a man needs all the friends he can get. No one can battle the continual dangers on his own. Even a fearless frontiersman like Nate King needs help now and then and he's always ready to give it when it's needed. So when an elderly Shoshone warrior comes to Nate asking for help, Nate agrees to lend a hand. The old warrior knows he doesn't have long to live and he wants to die in the remote canyon where his true love was killed many years before, slain by a giant bear straight out of Shoshone myth. No Shoshone will dare accompany the old warrior, so he and Nate will brave the dreaded canyon alone. And as Nate soon learns the hard way, some legends are far better left undisturbed.

___4862-0 $3.99 US/$4.99 CAN